Ocanas

MARIA LUISA

MARIA LUISA

by Winifred Madison

J. B. LIPPINCOTT COMPANY
Philadelphia and New York

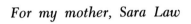

For my mother, Sara Law

MARIA LUISA

CHAPTER ONE

Late on a sunny afternoon toward the end of September, a bus made its way through the crowded streets of Oakland. After two days of traveling, the bus was dusty and the air inside smelled of orange peels and smoke. But the brown-skinned girl who sat with her nose pressed against the window hardly noticed the staleness of the bus. She was looking at the city with wide eyes as the bus rose on a highway which curved in the air like a ribbon of cement. It bumped along as well as it could while hordes of speeding cars raced past. The bus stopped briefly at a tollgate and finally rolled along the wide bridge that leads to San Francisco. Now she could see the city as it rose proudly above the blue water of the bay.

"*Dios mío*," she said to herself softly, "so it's really there after all!"

She nudged the little boy who lay half asleep on the seat beside her. He was tired of the trip, tired of asking, "When do we get there?" It was always the same answer. "Pretty soon."

9

"Look, Juan, wake up! There it is! San Francisco!"

It really was beautiful, she thought, even more so than the picture postcard Miss Summer, the teacher back in San Luis, had shown her. High buildings rose, one behind the other on hills steeper than any she had ever dreamed of. It was a white and sparkling city that seemed to float in the blue water like an island.

Juan was awake now and chattering with excitement.

"Boats, María Lusia, look, boats! So many of them. And a sailboat over there! See?"

The lady in front turned around and smiled at Juan who paid no attention whatever to her. He had never seen a real boat in all his life, and now there were more than he could count. They looked like big toys. Several steamers were making their way to sea and all over the bay sailboats leaned in the wind, sometimes catching the light of the setting sun. Brown and white seagulls glided through the air, but their cries couldn't be heard because the windows of the bus were closed.

To María Luisa who had grown up in San Luis, Arizona, where a few houses and shacks, a one-room school, a garage, and a restaurant clustered around a crossroad made up the whole town, San Francisco was like something in a dream. As the bus came close to the end of the bridge, the city seemed to grow enormous suddenly as though it could easily swallow the bus. It was all a little frightening. What made it even more exciting was the way the cars all rushed forward. Everything was happening too fast and María Luisa found she was holding her breath. San Luis had never been like this!

"We're almost there!" she thought. They had had almost thirty hours to get ready for this moment ever since they boarded the bus in San Luis, and now they had to rush to get ready to get off. Buy

Juan looked a little crumpled and not as clean as when he had left home. A lady on the bus had given him a chocolate bar and it had smeared on his shirt. María Luisa wet the corner of her handkerchief with her tongue and rubbed at the stain which wouldn't come off. She combed his thick black hair until it was neat and then, as she wiped his face with a Kleenex, she noticed tears threatening in his large dark eyes.

"You mustn't cry now," she whispered, "we'll be there soon. What will Aunt Rosa think if she sees you crying?"

She spoke to him in Spanish and he answered her, whimpering a little.

"I wanna go home, María Luisa; I wanna go where Mama is."

María Luisa found herself close to tears, too. But she couldn't give in to them. Not now, of all times!

"We can't go back, Juan. You know that. Besides we can't see Mama in the hospital; they won't let children in. We'll see her next summer. Remember, that's what they told us."

"But I don't wanna go to San Francisco. I wanna go home."

María Luisa understood all too well. Some of the shivers of excitement that seemed to dance up and down her back were shivers of fear. But Juan was a little boy, only six, and María Luisa couldn't let him know that she was frightened, too. So she acted as if she knew all about it.

"You're going to *like* it, Juan. You wait and see! It will be lots of fun. You'll have cousins to play with and we'll even see the Pacific Ocean. . . ."

She didn't finish the sentence as she was absorbed in giving herself one last critical look in her pocket mirror; it showed a brown face with large dark eyes, like Juan's. Her hair could stand a brushing, she decided, and she wished she had a clean blouse. Quickly she brushed back the shiny black hair and tied it at the nape of her neck with an elastic band and a red ribbon; now it looked better. But there was nothing much she could do about the blouse, not then.

The bus lurched sharply, pulled into the bus station, and stopped with a hiss. María Luisa took down her suitcase from the shelf.

"It's still in one piece," she told Juan. Sister Celeste, another of the teachers in San Luis, had told her it would take a miracle to hold the suitcase together all the way to San Francisco, but they still had to get to Aunt Rosa's house with it.

Everybody was moving toward the front. Juan held María Luisa's hand so tight it hurt. Looking out of the window, María Luisa thought there must be hundreds of people moving around in the station, and she felt a new panic start. How would she ever find Aunt Rosa in all that crowd?

Another terrifying thought struck her. What if Aunt Rosa weren't there? Then what would she do?

But Aunt Rosa will be there, she told herself firmly. She had written and promised. She had even said that she would be wearing a purple dress and a pin in the shape of a rose pinned to her shoulder so that María Luisa would be able to pick her out.

"If I find her in all this crowd," María Luisa thought, "that will be the miracle!"

She paused on the step of the bus and looked up and down the crowded line of people who stood waiting to greet the passengers. *Caray,* so many people were there and so many of them were moving about! It would be hopeless to find someone.

No sooner did she think that though, than she caught a glimpse of unmistakable purple and the glint of a gold pin on the shoulder. It was a city lady who wore it, a large woman with thick black hair brought up to the top of her head in a tidy, thick bun and golden earrings dangling from her ears. Aunt Rosa? It must be, for she seemed to recognize María Luisa, too, and waving, made her way through the crowd toward her.

With a torrent of Spanish endearments, she hugged and kissed María Luisa. Immediately her fears vanished; everything would be all right now. Aunt Rosa was about to pick up Juan and hug him, but his look warned her that he was too big a boy for that sort of treatment, so she bent down and embraced him instead.

"Juanito! Come, kiss your Aunt Rosa. That's it. Do you know there are two little boys waiting for you to come so they can play with you? They are your cousins. Did you know that?"

He nodded soberly and clung to María Luisa's skirt.

"Come, let's go," Aunt Rosa said, picking up the suitcase while María Luisa prayed for it to hold together until they reached home. "We have to catch the bus on Market Street. Everyone is waiting at home to see you."

María Luisa and Juan followed their aunt to the street. There were almost too many things to see all at once! People, cars, stores, signs, buildings, and of course María Luisa wanted to get a good look at Aunt Rosa, too. But she had to run, half dragging Juan, in order to keep up with Aunt Rosa who was hurrying to catch the bus. It stopped with a great hiss and squeak of brakes, and they all got on. Then they drove along the biggest avenue María Luisa had ever seen in her life.

"You have big eyes," Aunt Rosa said as she looked into her niece's face, "just like your mother!"

If María Luisa's eyes were big, it was because she wanted to see everything at once. Aunt Rosa kept asking questions, but the bus was so noisy, María Luisa could hardly hear her. At last, Aunt Rosa cried, "Come! We get off here!"

"How fast everybody moves!" María Luisa thought while they pushed their way to the front of the bus.

They walked up a hill. Many of the houses were painted in pastel colors and seemed enormous to María Luisa. Some of them, however, seemed a little sad and unpainted with an occasional window missing. María Luisa could hardly wait to see Aunt Rosa's house. At the corner of the block there was a small Mexican grocery store with strings of dried red chili peppers hanging inside and a big striped cat sleeping in the window. "It looks like the grocery in San Luis," María Luisa thought, and that was somehow comforting.

"This is our street," Aunt Rosa said as they turned the corner and walked up another hill.

CHAPTER TWO

It was the steepest street María Luisa had ever seen.
Even the cars were parked sideways, facing the curb, and
Aunt Rosa explained that if they were parked the usual
way, up and down, they were in danger of rolling down-
hill. In the next block the hill was so sharp that cars
couldn't go there at all and the paved street had been replaced by steps.

María Luisa had never seen such tall houses before.
They were at least three or four stories high, painted in
soft colors of gray, white, pink, or yellow. Impressed as
she was, María Luisa could not help noticing that many
of them were sadly in need of paint. Some of the alleys
between the houses were badly cluttered with old bicy-
cles and ashcans, but María Luisa noticed that sometimes
there were tiny little gardens trying to grow in front of
the houses. There were garages under the houses and the
steps leading up to the first floor of the houses sometimes
had black wrought-iron rails that formed beautiful pat-
terns or wooden rails with carved designs. There seemed

15

to be something special about each house, a pane of stained glass in a round window, or a porch decorated with fringes of carved wood that looked like the frosting on a cake, or a round section of the house that bulged out like a tower.

"You live in one of these houses?" María Luisa asked, forgetting her manners. "You must be rich!"

Aunt Rosa's laugh was full and throaty. "That's the very last thing we are—rich! We live in only one small part of the house. At one time rich people did live here, but now . . ." she sighed, "it's not the same. Here we are!"

María Luisa was glad because her arm was aching from pulling Juan along the uphill climb. They followed Aunt Rosa through a group of small children who stopped playing to stare at them, up stairs that led to a cream-colored house and then up a second flight of stairs that was dimly lit. Aunt Rosa flung open the door on a living room that seemed jammed with furniture and filled with people.

"Here they are!" she called out as she smiled at María Luisa and Juan. "Come in! This is your new home!"

There were shouts of welcome, a new hubbub of noise, and María Luisa felt that everyone was looking at her. No wonder Juan tried to hide his face in his sister's skirt. Someone grabbed the suitcase and at that moment it chose to open, spilling everything all over the floor— underwear, toothpaste, letter paper, nighties—everything. The miracle hadn't lasted quite long enough. María Luisa's face turned a burning red, as a chorus of sympathetic "oh's" greeted her along with a few good-humored jokes.

"You might as well smile. It's already happened!" Aunt Rosa said as she helped María Luisa stuff everything back hastily into the suitcase. All the while María Luisa was aware of all the noise in the room. A large clumsy-looking TV was blaring away, competing with a radio on which a Spanish program sputtered with as high a volume as the poor radio could manage. A toothless old lady in black sat with her ear next to the radio and grinned and nodded at the children. A boy was playing a guitar and everybody seemed to be talking at once, all in Spanish. Aunt Rosa began the introductions.

"This is your grandmother, *Abuelita!*" Aunt Rosa whispered to María Luisa. "Kiss her." María Luisa pressed her lips against the wrinkled cheeks of the frail old lady. Although she was her cousins' grandmother and not her own, still a grandmother was a grandmother.

The room also seemed to be full of little children. Too impatient to wait for introductions to their cousin, Roberto, who seemed to be about nine years old, and José, a plump little boy of six, came over to Juan. Everyone smiled when José put his arms around Juan and kissed him on the cheek. Juan blushed and looked at María Luisa as if to ask, "What do I do now?" But he seemed less frightened than he had been before.

"And this is Miguel, my son," Aunt Rosa announced proudly.

"Mike," corrected the handsome boy who had not stopped strumming his guitar for even a second. "Hello, María Luisa, hi, Juan! Glad to see you." He spoke in English.

He was perhaps sixteen or seventeen years old and María Luisa seemed to know right away that they would be friends, even if he was older than she. She smiled nervously and said, "Hi!"

The three stout ladies stitting on the sofa were neighbors or relatives. In all the confusion, María Luisa never quite decided which were which, but she nodded and smiled at each.

"And this is Elena, your cousin. You'll be good friends, yes?"

Elena! María Louisa had heard of her cousin, but she had never dreamed she would be so beautiful. "She could be on the cover of a magazine!" María Luisa thought as she stared at her, unable to say anything for a moment. Elena, younger than Mike but dressed to look older, was leaning back in an old overstuffed chair, calmly filing her nails. A lacy sweater of pale lavender and a silky violet skirt accented her light brown skin, long black curly hair, and dark eyes. She turned to María Luisa, looked her up and down quickly, said, "Hello," in a cool voice and went back to filing her nails.

María Luisa whispered back a subdued hello. She was overcome with Elena's beauty and yet disappointed that she had been so cool. She didn't seem at all glad to see me, María Luisa thought. Maybe later on she would be more friendly. . . .

María Luisa felt someone tugging at her skirt. Looking down she saw a baby grinning up at her and as María Luisa smiled back at her, she became excited and danced up and down so hard that her diaper fell off. Aunt Rosa picked her up to a small chorus of cheers while the baby laughed and waved. It was clear that everyone was a bit silly over that baby. "This is Rosita! Now you know everyone. Wait, not yet, I almost forgot. There's one more. Emilio!" Her voice rang out loud and clear.

"I'm coming," a rich baritone voice called back. Then Uncle Emilio came into the room. At the moment he was tying a narrow black silk tie over a richly embroidered Mexican wedding shirt. María Luisa stared at that and at his woven belt, black pants, and highly polished shoes. He looked so dressed up that she wondered if he were going to a party. His black hair, gray at the edges, had been carefully combed and smelled of a man's scent. He bent down to kiss María Luisa, his black mustache brushing against her cheek.

"So this is the María Luisa Santos I've heard so much about and this is Juan Santos! Welcome to the Nuñez family! Now you are one of us."

Juan wanted to say something but Uncle Emilio had to bend down to hear him.

"We're going to be here for only a little while. My mother will get better soon."

"Well, of course your mother will get better soon! In the meantime, wouldn't you like to be in our family?"

Juan looked at María Luisa with some alarm, but at her reassuring expression he looked back at Uncle Emilio and said, "All right," very softly. He would do it for a little while, but not forever. He could not tear his eyes from his uncle. He'd never seen such elegant clothes, the short red jacket over the embroidered shirt and the satin band along the outside seam of his uncle's pants. Was this how people dressed in San Francisco?

Smiling at their confusion, Uncle Emilio explained.

"You didn't expect an uncle who would look like a

street musician . . . a *mariachi*, did you? Well, I'm not one, but I come close. I'm a waiter, and this is how we dress."

Aunt Rosa interrupted. "But, Emilio, you give them the wrong idea. Not all waiters dress like that. Your uncle works in very beautiful Mexican restaurant. Such a place you've never seen!" she said, moving her head from side to side as though she couldn't begin to explain how elegant it was.

"You should see it," Roberto piped up. "It's got big carved doors and at night there are torches outside and lots of candles inside. . . ."

"Do you go there too?" María Luisa asked Roberto, surprised. Now her eyes lit up. Maybe Uncle Emilio would take her there sometime!

"I would like to see it," she told Uncle Emilio, meaning to be politely interested, but hoping he would remember and take her there.

Everyone laughed and María Luisa found herself getting red. She wished she hadn't said anything and she couldn't understand what was so funny about what she had said.

"It's a Mexican restaurant," Mike explained, "but nobody ever said it was for Chicanos. They couldn't afford a glass of water there, that is, if they could get by the front door."

"I don't know about *that*," Elena said tartly. "I *know* people who have gone there."

"Sure," Uncle Emilio said with some sarcasm, "you know such people. Like the President of Mexico or the ambassador or a movie star. We let them come in, sure. As for the Nuñez family . . ."

He was interrupted by a loud insistent honking of an automobile horn downstairs. How he managed to hear it with all the other noise in the room was a mystery, but Uncle Emilio heard it. He kissed everybody good-bye and spoke to María Luisa and Juan once more. "I want you to be very happy here and to feel that this is your home."

Then he looked at his own children and spoke more sternly. "And it's up to you to see that you all get along together. Or else . . ." He held up a warning finger and then hurried down the stairs.

That seemed to be a signal for everyone to leave. The neighbors and the sister-in-law left; the grandmother went to her room; Mike disappeared; the boys took Juan to their bedroom to show him their toys and Aunt Rosa took Rosita into the kitchen, all the time muttering that she must make dinner because the poor lambs must be hungry after that long trip.

And so María Luisa found herself left alone in the living room. Then she realized that Elena was still there and now she was staring directly at María Luisa.

CHAPTER THREE

"How old are you?" she asked.

"Twelve, almost thirteen."

"I'd say you were about ten."

María Luisa gulped. "I've been through the sixth grade," she said defensively.

Elena had spoken with a trace of scorn, not kindly but not unkindly either. María Luisa was instantly ashamed of the white blouse and dark skirt she wore. In San Luis it had always seemed the perfect thing to wear to school or at home, but now it seemed childish and unfashionable. The smart stockings and shoes that seemed so fashionable on Elena's slender legs made María Luisa want to hide the scuffy, brown matter-of-fact shoes on her own feet.

But Elena wasn't perfect. She was chewing bubble gum, making loud snapping noises as she blew out huge bubbles. Sister Celeste had never let any of the students chew bubble gum in her presence; she considered it crude. For a moment María Luisa took comfort in the fact that Elena wasn't ideal. In the next moment, however, Elena stretched and yawned and it didn't seem to matter if she chewed gum or not. She really was beautiful, and when she moved, she was like a graceful cat.

"Come on. I'll show you where you'll be sleeping and you can put your things away," she said.

María Luisa picked up the shabby suitcase and followed Elena to a small room at the end of the hall.

"It's a wonder we could fit a bed in here for you," she complained. "It was crowded enough before."

That was clear enough. A small chest of drawers and a scarred pink chair had been crowded together to make room for María Luisa's bed. At the foot of her bed, which was little more than a rough wooden cot, there was a small trunk covered with an old hand-woven blanket, a *sarape* that must have come from the old country.

"That's Grandmother's trunk," Elena said as though she loathed it, "but *I* have to keep it in here with that precious rag on top."

For the first time María Luisa knew what it was to be a poor relative. If Grandmother's trunk could upset Elena so, what must she think of a cousin moving in.

"I'm sorry to be in your way, Elena. But we're going to leave in June. My mother will be all better then."

"How do you know?" Elena asked tartly. María Luisa was alarmed at this question. Perhaps Elena knew something she didn't know. Perhaps Miss Summer had known but had not dared to tell the children that their mother would not get well. But Sister Celeste had said they must never doubt for a minute but that God in His goodness could work any miracle . . . one had to believe . . . Sister Celeste had been comforting.

"I know she'll get well. I know it, that's all," María Luisa answered with a firmness that seemed to quiet Elena.

"OK, OK, I just asked. Anyway, it's not your fault. You can't help it. Here, you can put your clothes in the closet, if you want to," she said as she handed María Luisa two wire hangers.

"I won't take up much room," María Luisa promised. "All I have is my good dress for church, and what I have on now."

She shook out the wrinkles from her one good dress, a simple blue cotton one, and gave the unused hanger back to Elena. As María Luisa hung her dress in the closet she almost gasped to see how many dresses and blouses and sweaters Elena seemed to have. And shoes too! They practically covered the floor.

"*Dios mío*, you have lots of clothes!"

"Not so many. It just seems that way to you. My mother says my father spoils me. But he likes to see me dressed up," Elena said. María Luisa thought how nice it would be to have a father who liked to see his daughter all dressed up.

"Want to see something?" Elena asked. Then without waiting for an answer, she took out a soft clingy dress with a jeweled collar. She stroked it as she showed it to María Luisa. She was certainly proud of her clothes, María Luisa thought, and no wonder.

"Oooooh, it's so soft and lovely!" she exclaimed as she touched it. She marveled at the jeweled collar. Now that Elena had proof of her cousin's admiration, she became a little kinder toward her.

"I'll show you my new cape," she said, as though she were doing María Luisa a great favor, but as she reached into the closet to get it, Aunt Rosa's voice came from the kitchen.

"Elena, come set the table. Your cousins must be hungry, so come quickly now. Tonight we use the tablecloth in honor of their coming today."

Elena made a face and rolled her eyes, while María Luisa looked down. She was very uncomfortable and felt very guilty. She hadn't asked for the tablecloth or for Elena to set the table, and yet because of her and Juan, Elena had to go to all this trouble.

Elena sauntered over to the kitchen shelves as slowly as she possibly could, as if it were beneath her dignity to help in the kitchen. María Luisa stood in the doorway and watched, not knowing what to do. Aunt Rosa bustled around, stopping to stir something in a pot that smelled delicious and at the same time yelling to the boys to get washed. Carelessly Elena pulled down plates from the shelf.

"Here, let me help you," María Luisa cried. Without a word or a second's delay, Elena placed the pile of plates in her cousin's arms so fast it was a miracle they did not drop. As María Luisa set them around the dining-room table, Elena came in and threw the silverware down in a heap as though she expected María Luisa to set it out.

"I wouldn't mind doing it at all," María Luisa thought, "if only she talked to me. If only she liked me a little. . . . Maybe she will after a while," she comforted herself.

But at that moment she would have given anything to be back in the tiny kitchen in San Luis with her mother.

25

CHAPTER FOUR

That night when María Luisa finally went to bed she was too tired to tell if she was happy or sad in her new home. But she did know one thing—she was bewildered by the Nuñez family. "It's so different," she kept thinking, and indeed it was different from anything she had ever known. Up to now she had lived with her mother and Juan; it was quiet and pleasant and nothing much seemed to happen. Now she was part of an enormous family ranging from little Rosita to the ancient grandmother. Everyone seemed to lead an exciting life. Everyone had something to say. She was overwhelmed by the noise as much as anything else.

They had all sat around the oval dining-room table and it was clear that the tablecloth, well worn but still very white, signified that this was a special occasion. Everyone seemed to talk and laugh at the same time. Juan had lost his shyness and was giggling with Roberto and José as though they had always known one another. Indeed he felt so much at home that when José pretended to make a highway through his rice and drive a tiny toy car through it, Juan did the same. María Luisa frowned at him and shook her head, hoping he would stop; she felt the full responsibility for the way he behaved. But Aunt Rosa had more practice in bringing up little boys. All she had to do was look at them, make a tsk-tsk sound, and they stopped.

"More chicken, María Luisa? We made it special for you. Another enchilada maybe? Your mother used to make it like this, didn't she? Only you don't eat much. You're so thin. Here!"

They piled her plate with food and she cried, "No, please, no!" She could never eat that much. Besides, she was busy listening to all the conversations. Elena seemed a little mean as she kidded Mike, but her eyes twinkled.

"You should see this girl who is so crazy about Mike. She ran after him down the hall today. . . ."

"Darn you, Elena, cool it."

But Elena went on. "She's blond and her hair goes out like this, and she weighs only two hundred pounds." She puffed out her cheeks and acted in such a way that María Luisa felt she knew exactly what the girl was like. Elena was clever. "And the only way Mike could get away from her was to go . . ."

"Never mind," Aunt Rosa said, bringing this teasing to a stop. "Leave Mike alone now."

It must have been a running family joke. Mike did not look altogether unhappy that the girls liked him or even that Elena kidded him about it. Roberto tried to tell a joke in his high little-boy's voice, and although the joke was not very good, his gestures and expressions were so funny that María Luisa found herself laughing hard. All

27

of the Nuñezes seemed to have a way of acting, as though they could easily be on the stage putting on a show.

When dinner was over, Elena said she was going to the movies with her friend, Connie.

"Oh, no," Aunt Rosa protested. "Leave your cousin all alone on her first night here? That's not nice. You know better than that. Besides, it's your turn to do dishes."

"But I already promised I'd go. . . ."

"It's all right," María Luisa said quickly, afraid that Elena would resent her all the more if she had to stay home with her. "I can do the dishes. I don't mind at all."

"No, she should stay home on your first night here," Aunt Rosa insisted, as she grew more and more irritated with Elena. But if María Luisa had expected Elena would insist on doing the dishes herself and being with her cousin on her very first night, which was what María Luisa would most certainly have done if the situation were reversed, she was in for a disappointment.

"Oh, Mama, I'll do it tomorrow. I mean I *promised* Connie. Anyway, you don't care, do you, María Luisa? See, Mama, she doesn't mind at all."

Aunt Rosa shook her head, displeased with her daughter, but María Luisa began to clear the table and scrape the dishes to show that she didn't mind at all. Elena was humming in the other room as she changed her clothes. While María Luisa piled the dishes, Mike walked into the kitchen. He too had changed his clothes and was now dressed in tight blue velvet pants and a flowered satin shirt. My heavens, María Luisa thought, what a family this is for getting dressed up.

"The combo's playing at the Roc tonight, and we'll probably get home late," he told his mother as he polished his shoes.

"What's a combo?" María Luisa asked him in a soft, hesitant voice. Although all of the Nuñez family spoke Spanish, they used many words that María Luisa had never heard before.

Roberto snickered at María Luisa's question, but Mike explained patiently that a combo was a rock 'n' roll group with guitar, drums, double bass, and trumpet. Mike played the guitar, of course, and sometimes sang. He also explained to María Luisa that the "Roc" was a night club where they played, and implied by a gesture that it wasn't the finest place in San Francisco.

"It's a hole. I wish you could hear the combo, María Luisa, but I couldn't take you to a place like that, even if you were old enough to go. It's a beginning for us, though. You have to play wherever you can when you're starting."

"But I think it's wonderful," María Luisa said. "Some-day you will be a famous guitar player. Everyone will be proud of you and pay lots of money to come hear you."

What made her say such a thing? What did she know of music? Almost nothing. Yet Mike had a way of speaking and moving that made her think he would be very good.

He watched her as she scoured away a burned spot on one of the cooking pots. "Listen, María Luisa, be careful with Elena. Don't let her push all her work off on you, because she'll be only too willing to do it. If she gives you a hard time about anything, come and tell me. OK? You hear?"

She smiled at him and nodded. She wasn't likely to run to anyone to complain about Elena, but it was good to know that Mike wanted to protect her.

"I gotta go now. Good night," he cried and then left.

Soon Aunt Rosa and María Luisa were alone in the kitchen. Aunt Rosa was washing the dishes and María Luisa was drying them carefully.

"The kitchen is always the best place to talk," Aunt Rosa said. "And now that we have a few minutes, you must tell me all about your mother. Everything."

Aunt Rosa asked many questions and María Luisa had to recall everything for her, even things she had wanted to forget. She told her aunt how her father had died two years ago when the truck he was driving fell into a ravine, turning over and over and finally burning up.

"Then my mother worked in a restaurant and then they found she had TB and so she couldn't work any more."

It was painful to remember it all over again. The words she spoke were few, but it was as though she were living it all over again. She recalled just how it was when she and Juan said good-bye to their mother when she left for the sanitarium, and how the doctor had assured Miss Summer, with María Luisa worried and tense as she stood there listening, that in eight months Mrs. Santos would be as good as new. Now it seemed years ago, although it was only a few days, that Miss Summer and Sister Celeste had helped María Luisa pack a suitcase, had taken them to their house for dinner, given them a little money and much advice, and had put them on the bus to San Francisco.

"Such a sad story! Poor girl!" said Aunt Rosa as she put two soapy arms around María Luisa and held her close. María Luisa didn't like being a "poor girl," which came too close to being a poor relation, but even so, Aunt Rosa's strong arms were comforting. It was funny how a touch of a hand, an understanding look, and a soft voice could make one feel better.

Later María Luisa helped bathe the little boys. They played with plastic toy boats in the water and became so excited about a race, splashing the water everywhere and giggling so hard, that soon María Luisa found herself laughing along with them.

Even after they had said their prayers and the light in the bedroom was turned out, María Luisa lay awake in her new bed and heard the boys' snickering. It grew fainter and fainter and then stopped as they fell asleep. María Luisa fell asleep, too.

A blinding light from the unshaded lamp flashed on and woke María Luisa up. Elena had come in and was undressing.

"Oh, did I wake you? I almost forgot you were here."

"It's all right. Did you have a good time?" María Luisa was only being polite. She wished that Elena would turn the light off and let her get back to sleep. Too late she realized she'd made a mistake in asking about the good time; Elena was ready to talk all night. She sat on the edge of her bed and rubbed cream on her face.

"Promise not to tell my folks? We had a blast. What a *time!* I met this boy, Tony, and we went for a ride on his Honda. My father would kill me if he knew. But he doesn't know. Tony and I went to the beach . . ."

"You said you were going to the movies with Connie."

"She couldn't go. I just sorta bumped into Tony. . . ." the sentence drifted as she began to brush her hair. "Didn't you have any boy friends in whatzis, San Luis?"

"Who, me? No, I guess not. I mean all the kids played together. It wasn't like boy friends and girl friends, not like it is here."

"I have lots of friends," Elena sighed as she stopped

brushing her hair long enough to put on a filmy yellow nightgown. She began to comb her hair once more. *Caray*, María Luisa thought, she's going to comb it all night. Elena kept talking about the good time she had had and then at last, she turned out the light.

But now María Luisa was wide awake and could not sleep. Why should she feel so sad and so alone? She sat up in bed so she could look out the window. But all she could see was blackness where the house next door blocked out all the view except for a long sliver of light that gave María Luisa a glimpse of the city below. In this limited view, she saw bright lights, colored signs flashing on and off, and strings of moving red and white lights as an endless parade of cars went up and down the streets. This city was so enormous it made her feel very small.

Thoughts of San Luis kept coming back to her, silly things she remembered like the little canary in the cage that her father had nailed to the front of the house. She saw herself, a little girl sitting contentedly on the back stoop with a cat rubbing against her leg while her mother sang as she scrubbed clothes in a round washtub that stood in the backyard under an olive tree. That was where she belonged, not here where in only a few hours she had learned to become ashamed of her blouse and skirt, of never having had a boy friend, and of not knowing what a combo was. She wasn't even sure what a Honda was although she guessed it was probably a motorcycle. How she hated an ignorance she never knew she had before that day! Juan had been right when he wanted to go home earlier that day. If only she were back in San Luis, she would never complain again.

"María Luisa, what's the matter? Are you crying?"

Elena sounded surprised. María Luisa had tried to muffle the sounds of her weeping but instead she had awakened her cousin. Now, she thought, Elena really will be annoyed. But she did not know her as well as she thought. Elena sat up in bed for a few moments looking at her little cousin who was trying to check her tears, and then on an impulse came over and sat on the bed beside her. Like some people, she might tease but could not bear to hear anyone cry. Now her voice was soft and concerned.

"You're homesick, aren't you?"

María Luisa sniffed and nodded. Elena brought her some Kleenex.

"Poor kid! I guess it must be strange to leave your home. I don't think I'd cry if I ever left home, but maybe you're different."

"When I said I didn't want you in my room, I didn't really mean it, María Luisa. It will be fun having you, like having a sister. See?"

She was using the same kind of cheeriness that María Luisa used when she wanted to comfort Juan, not exactly sincere but comforting, like whistling in the dark.

"Hey. You're not so bad-looking. It's just that you have San Luis written all over you. You really are a country girl, you know? I'd like to brush out your hair; I know a good way for you to wear it. Maybe I can give you some dresses; we can shorten them for you. I have a red woollen jumper that would look fine on you."

Now Elena was getting enthusiastic as she saw María Luisa in a new light, an ugly duckling to be transformed. She wanted María Luisa to try on dresses then and there. María Luisa sat up in bed and the tears dried on her face as she watched her cousin turn on the blinding light once more and begin to look through her closet. She could not understand her impulsive cousin and this sudden affection astonished her. At the same time she was fired with new hope; with Elena's help she would no longer be such a poor relation but a good friend.

It wasn't to happen that night, however. Aunt Rosa heard the girls and called out to them to go to sleep, for heaven's sake, didn't they know they had to get up early the next day.

This time María Luisa slept soundly and did not wake up until the sun beamed across her face the next morning.

CHAPTER FIVE

"A picnic, María Luisa! We're going on a picnic!" Juan sang it out in a happy singsong voice, although he didn't really know what a picnic was. The word was beautiful to María Luisa, too; her father had often promised that he would take the family on a big picnic to a place where they would all go on a merry-go-round and a Ferris wheel. Afterward they would sit on the grass and eat lunch while a band played music; he promised them big bags of popcorn and fluffy, pink spun-sugar cones. However, it was always a promise. He had never actually taken them, and then it was too late.

Aunt Rosa had announced at breakfast that they were all going to take a holiday and have a picnic in Golden Gate Park that very day. Uncle Emilio said it was a great idea and asked María Luisa if she didn't think it was a great pity that he had to work and could not go. "I wish you would be there," she said shyly, and that seemed to please him.

Later that day the whole family, except Uncle Emilio, climbed on the bus. There was Aunt Rosa with a picnic basket, Mike, Elena, María Luisa who held the baby, Roberto, José, Juan, and even the little grandmother who trailed behind but was determined to get on the bus with everyone else. The bus went up and down the hills and every once in a while, as it crossed a street, María Luisa caught sight of the blue water of the Bay in the distance and the bridge they had crossed the day before. It spread out like a long silver thread and it was impossible to imagine that cars, trucks, and buses could all fit on that slender line.

"What do you think of San Francisco now?" Aunt Rosa asked.

"Oh, I love it. I really do. It's so beautiful," she said.

Elena snorted. "Sure. Just wait till you go to school here! Then we'll see how much you love it."

"But I like school," María Luisa protested. "Why shouldn't I like it here?"

Elena wore that odd one-sided smile that bothered

35

María Luisa; it was as though María Luisa amused her.

"This isn't like San Luis," she said distinctly without trying to disguise her contempt for it.

"Don't mind her," Mike said. "She's jealous. She's always jealous."

"I'm not, darn you, I'm *not*," Elena hissed at him and stuck out her tongue. But she squeezed María Luisa's hand as though to say, "Don't feel hurt. I'm just kidding."

"Here, behave yourselves. We're at the park now," Aunt Rosa said. They all got off the bus, leaving it quite empty.

"I've never seen such a place as this," María Luisa confided to Mike as they walked through the park. Somehow it was all right to tell things to Mike, but she was still a little afraid of Elena's sharp tongue. "Heaven must be like this. All these trees, and look at those flowers there!"

Now it was Mike's turn to smile. "You think it's like heaven? Wait till you know it a little better."

"In San Luis we had nothing like this. Those big green spaces and these trees. *Dios mío*, they are so big!"

They walked to a grove where eucalyptus and pine trees grew, and set the lunch box on a picnic table. Music from the merry-go-round drifted up the hill to the picnic grove.

"Do you want to go on it?" Mike asked.

María Luisa's eyes shone with the answer, a resplendent yes!

Aunt Rosa stayed behind while all the children ran down the hill. Mike was so amused with Juan's excitement that he bought a whole string of tickets so everyone could ride. Juan danced up and down and María Luisa, no less excited, said little but felt as though she would burst with happiness.

She sat on a black horse with a proud black head and a jeweled harness. The roof above had been made of fitted pieces of colored glass and the reflections kept coloring the horses and the riders pink, green, yellow, and blue. The music was a little rusty and many of the notes seemed to be missing; the merry-go-round creaked; and the oval mirrors which reflected the riders were wavy, like something seen in a dream. María Luisa sat proud and tall on the horse as it rose up and down on its circular trip. From time to time she was aware of Mike's dark profile and the faces of the children waiting for their turn. The world outside the merry-go-round no longer existed; this ride would go on forever.

But the music slowed down while the carrousel moved more slowly and finally stopped. Mike stood by her horse and looked up at her.

"We have to get off now," he said.

"I never want to get off. I could stay here forever," María Luisa said. She made a little sigh of regret. Mike helped her off. Then they all walked back up the hill.

"You really are nothing but a little kid, a hick, an *inocente*," Elena said as they sat around the table eating lunch. María Luisa, basking in the sun with a taco in one hand and a bottle of orange pop in the other, stared dreamily down below at the playground where children played on swings, climbed on the jungle gyms, and ran over to play on the old worn-out cable car that had been placed at the far end of the playground for children to play on. Pigeons were wheeling through the air and everyone down below seemed happy.

"You really are a country cousin," Elena went on.

"So what if I am?" María Luisa snapped, annoyed that anyone would want to spoil such a beautiful day. "What about it? Shouldn't I like to be here?"

Elena smirked. "You think everything is wonderful! Everything is beautiful! Life is just perfect! What an idiot you are!"

María Luisa wondered if she really was an idiot. Why did Elena pick on her so, especially when she'd been so nice last night when she found her crying? Anyway, María Luisa had never said life was perfect and everything was wonderful. Never in all this world!

After lunch the grandmother took a nap and Aunt Rosa took out her knitting. Elena put on dark glasses and sat in the sun. The little boys had long ago run down to the playground. "Let's go," Mike said to María Luisa, and the two of them strolled down to the playground to the parallel bars. Mike began to show off some of the tricks he knew while María Luisa watched him lazily. Her attention was drawn to a commotion on the swings.

A fight seemed to be going on, a fight that was becoming more and more intense. Somehow Juan had stumbled into the midst of it and one of the big boys had knocked him down. Immediately María Luisa ran over to rescue him.

"*Gabachos!* Bullies! Cut that out. Leave my brother alone. He's just a little kid!"

She tore at one of the boys in an effort to get to Juan and help him up. She continued to shout in Spanish, of course, as if anyone could remember to speak English at a time like this. Besides she was angry. Miss Summer had

38

always warned her to watch her temper, but when Juan was in danger of being hurt, she had no time to think of that.

One of the boys who had been fighting became aware of her, looked at her and laughed.

"Hey, anyone want a Spanish lesson?" he cried, and then he pushed María Luisa. Furious, she pounded at him with her fists and kicked his shins. Somewhere she saw the flash of a knife, and then she felt Mike pulling her back and away from the fracas.

"Cool it, you punks!" he yelled as he reached for Juan and managed to pull him back out of danger. There was nothing soft or sensitive about his voice now. One of the boys looked past Mike and saw a policeman on a horse at the edge of the playground. "Beat it, the fuzz!" he shouted. Within a few seconds the boys had disappeared and the fight was over.

María Luisa went over to Juan and knelt by him, putting her arms around him. He did not look as hurt as he looked puzzled. "Why did they hit me? I was only playing. I was waiting for my turn."

"Aw, come on, it happens all the time. You'll get over it," Mike said, cool and sophisticated about the whole incident, as though he had seen it many times before. The boys ran off. Apparently Juan was able to shrug off the whole affair, for in no time at all he was shouting happily as he slid down a huge corkscrew slide.

María Luisa was still puzzled. "Why did they pick on a little kid like Juan? He wouldn't hurt anyone. I don't understand."

"Some kids are bad characters. Some of them would be OK if they didn't get pushed around. School stinks, they drop out, they can't get a job, some of them are on acid. It's not always easy. So if you get pushed around, you feel better if you push someone else around. It don't make sense but that's how it is," Mike said.

"I see," María Luisa answered. But she did not really see how anyone could be so mean as to pick on little children. That such things could happen made the park a little less beautiful than it had been before.

"Mama, can you imagine, María Luisa has never seen the ocean?" Mike could not get over it.

"That's right. I'll never forget the first time I saw it," Aunt Rosa said. "It was so big. I was never so thrilled."

Mike and María Luisa had talked of it and now María Luisa felt she could not wait to see it. Aunt Rosa understood.

"Mike, why don't you take María Luisa for a little walk so she can see what it looks like. It isn't so far away. Then you can take the bus home later on."

María Luisa blushed and wished Aunt Rosa hadn't asked Mike. Perhaps he didn't want to be bothered with his country cousin any more than Elena did, and then he would resent her.

"Sure, c'mon," he said, just like that, without hesitating at all! María Luisa was astounded; he really was almost like a big brother. She kissed Aunt Rosa good-bye and then walked away with Mike.

"I wouldn't take you," he said, "only I liked the way you lit into that guy and yelled at him. I didn't think you were such a wildcat. That's OK. You gotta be tough to survive around here."

He seemed to have been amused by her outburst, but he admired it, too. María Luisa smiled to herself. A bad temper wasn't always such a bad thing to have.

They walked through the park and came to an extremely wide road. They crossed it and walked along the sidewalk that bordered the beach. The salty wind blew their hair about and María Luisa shivered a little. Soon they came to steps that led to the beach. They climbed down and walked through the sand beside the water. María Luisa's reactions were just like Aunt Rosa's. "It's so big!" she said at least three times, and she could think of little else to say because it really was so much bigger than anything she had imagined.

They stopped to watch the waves. Every now and then an enormous one would roll up to a huge crest as far along the coast as the eye could see, and then would burst into a long line of churning white foam which grew smaller and gentler as it came toward the shore. Little flocks of sandpipers walked rapidly up and down the edge of the water in hopes of finding food in each wave. In the distance another wave began to rise to a huge green crest.

The cousins walked in silence while the cold wind blew ripples in their clothes. It was hard to talk because the water roared constantly. Besides, Mike seemed to have withdrawn into his own thoughts. So he, too, could be a dreamer, María Luisa noticed. She wanted to ask him what he was thinking, but it would have been too forward. Thoughts could be very involved, as hard to describe as the ocean. How many times had she had thoughts she could not put into words!

41

From time to time she picked up a shell for Juan or a seagull feather. She could not get over it that one could find such treasures just lying about in the sand.

At last the wind seemed to die down for a little while and it was possible to talk.

"Do you really think you'll be happy here?" Mike asked. "Even after what happened in the park?"

"It was silly for me to expect everything to be perfect. *Caray*, even in San Luis not everything is perfect. So it's not perfect, but it's good. Your family is so nice to us, I am thankful."

"Well, you got a lot to learn. Listen, María Luisa, be careful with Elena."

"Oh?" What did he mean by that?

"When I said she was jealous before, I wasn't kidding. So watch it."

"But she's not jealous of me, for heaven's sake! What's there to be *jealous* of? Besides, she's so pretty, I've never seen such a beautiful girl."

"She's OK sometimes," Mike said and then shut his mouth. End of that conversation.

The sun was flooding the sky over the Pacific with a spreading pink light and the people on the beach became moving silhouettes. In the distance a little dog ran joyfully.

"When I see all this, it's so wonderful it seems to fill me up. Not just the good things but everything as it is, even that fight this afternoon. I want to put it all in words, to make it into a poem or a story. Do you think I'm crazy to want to do this?" María Luisa asked.

"Do you feel that way, too?" Mike asked. "When I see things I want to put them down, too, only I'd rather

42

make songs out of them. Music and words. My father thinks I'm nuts, absolutely crazy. We fight about it sometimes, so mostly I keep my ideas to myself. Sometimes they get so great I think I'll bust, so then I write them down, but not where anyone knows about it."

So Mike understood. It made María Luisa feel less alone now. It was something one couldn't tell just anybody, not even Elena or Aunt Rosa, kind as she was.

Mike changed the subject in one fast switch.

"Hey, do you like to run?"

"Sure. Do you?"

They ran along the beach for a long time until they were laughing and out of breath. Then Mike looked at his watch. Time to go home. He had to play with his combo that night.

"How far are we from home?" María Luisa asked as they ran toward the bus. Then she realized that when she spoke of "home" she did not mean San Luis at all, but San Francisco. She hadn't been there twenty-four hours and already it had become "home."

CHAPTER SIX

Sunday night María Luisa knelt on the floor of her room and using *Abuelita's* trunk as a desk, tried to write a letter. She bit the end of her pencil and two lines formed a frown on her forehead. Writing poems or stories had never given her too much trouble, but this letter to her mother was not quite so easy. Sister Celeste, who had given her the stationery and stamped envelopes, had said she must write a "happy" letter to her mother each week, for that would keep her from worrying and help her get well faster. María Luisa had promised soberly. If only her mother would get well. . . .

This was the problem. If she wrote a letter that was "too happy" and full of the good times she and Juan were having, perhaps her mother, lying alone in the hospital, would think her children did not miss her. Yet if she confessed to the fears and doubts that seemed to nibble at the edges of her new life, then her mother would worry. No, it would be best to write only cheerful things.

With that settled in her mind, she wrote the letter, in Spanish, of course, so that her mother could read it.

Dear Mama:

I hope you are feeling better now. Everyone here is well and sends love to you.

Today we went to church, early Mass. It is a big church and everything is in Spanish, the way it is back home.

Yesterday we went to Golden Gate Park to have a picnic. You would like it very much. It is very beautiful with green grass and lots of trees and flowers. Later Mike and I walked by the ocean. It is very big.

Juan is very happy and plays with his cousins. We both miss you and will be happy to see you again.

Your loving daughter,
María Luisa

She read over the letter and shook her head doubtfully. How could she possibly explain to her mother what her new life was like when everything in San Francisco was so different from San Luis?

She turned out the dim light and curled up in her bed. Staring dreamily at the strip of city lights, she thought of all the things she hadn't written down. So much had happened since she had come! There was that first glimpse of the city from the bridge; she had never seen so many tall buildings. And then the intense greenness of the park with its trees and grass was such a contrast to the flat rolling lands of Arizona. There it seemed one could look out forever over the land, but here one could do the same thing looking out over the Pacific Ocean. Poor San Luis suffered when it was compared to San Francisco.

Only San Francisco was disturbing, too. It had been

easier to sleep in San Luis. Here she lay awake remembering the fight in the park and the flash of the knife. People here were not easy to understand. For all his friendliness, Mike had seemed to draw into his own thoughts like a snail into its shell as they walked along the beach. There was Elena, too, scornful one minute and sugar-sweet the next.

She stretched out on the bed. Her eyes became heavy and she was soon asleep, only to be awakened abruptly by the sound of Elena humming and the light snapping on and glaring in her face. *Caray*, was it going to be like this every night?

At the moment Elena was admiring herself in the mirror over the bureau. She tossed back her mane of thick black hair and posed, pleased with herself. Obviously she had forgotten all about her cousin until she caught her eye in the mirror. Immediately the pose stopped; then she shrugged her shoulders and smiled, not really caring that she had been caught. She knew she was good-looking. There was no point denying it. Besides, it was obvious that this cousin of hers admired her. She held María Luisa's gaze in the mirror and then turned around, a new thought in her mind.

"You just like to sit and think, don't you? Well, *don't* you? Of course you do." María Luisa looked at her and said nothing. There was the slightest trace of scorn in her voice, but it mingled with a friendly confidence.

"You really are different, María Luisa. Did you know that?"

María Luisa shook her head. Different? In what way? Was this good? The way Elena put it, it was a fault.

"You ought to try to be more like other people," Elena said.

María Luisa sighed. She would never please her cousin, never.

"I think I'll go to sleep, if you don't mind," she said, turning to face the wall. But though her eyes were closed, it was a long time before she fell asleep.

CHAPTER SEVEN

Polishing Juan's shoes to a brilliant shine late that night, María Luisa realized that she was worried about school. She had seen her cousins look at each other and smile when she said that she just loved school in San Luis. Miss Summer had been the very best teacher and Sister Celeste, who had taught music and art, had been so kind. If it had been so splendid in a little place like San Luis, then surely a San Francisco school would be a hundred times better. How they had laughed!

"You're laughing at me. What's the matter? Do the teachers beat you or something?"

"You'll find out soon enough, so don't worry," Mike had said.

"The teachers won't beat you," Elena said, "but it's a drag, something you have to do. You can quit when you're eighteen. Lots of kids drop out before that, but my father won't let me."

All this talk made María Luisa nervous. She had washed and ironed her own clothes and Juan's, had made sure that he was well bathed and his hair and fingernails clean. Then she washed her own long black hair and when it was dry, brushed it until it shone. "At least we can look nice," she had comforted herself. Then she took out the two envelopes that contained her school records and information about Juan; Miss Summer had said these should be given to the school principals on the first day of school. She put them by her bed so she wouldn't forget them.

Monday morning brought in a thick fog. All the sunshine of the weekend seemed to have vanished forever. Aunt Rosa was taking Juan to the elementary school and she asked Elena to walk with María Luisa to the junior high school even though Elena herself went to the senior high school.

"I can't, Mama, not with all the homework I have to finish before school."

Aunt Rosa put her foot down. "That much you can do for your cousin," she said, and in the end Elena walked María Luisa to the junior high school. "I'd take you in to the office, but I'm afraid I'll be late," she said, and María Luisa felt more alone than ever as Elena walked away without looking back.

It was terrifying to have to walk into a new school with so many kids around. Well, she'd better go anyway. The office was just inside the front door. She entered timidly and whispered to the secretary that she was a new student, but she spoke too softly and had to repeat what she had said. The secretary told her to sit down on one of the hard chairs that lined the walls. Other children were sitting there already, almost as many as went to San Luis' single school. She wondered if they were all new students, like herself. There was certainly a great deal of variety among them and she could hardly keep from staring. There were black students, white students, a few Orientals, and many brown-skinned children like herself; there were also three who seemed so unusual that María Luisa wondered what they were.

Why, in San Luis there were only eighteen students, but they had known each other all their lives. To sit and not talk with each other would have been unthinkable to any of them. Maybe these children were all new, like herself. In the halls outside, masses of children seemed to move along. *Caray,* this was one big school, that was certain!

A bell rang and the children in the halls disappeared into the classrooms. A tall gentleman with pale blue eyes stepped into the office, looked around and then crooked his finger at María Luisa, motioning to her to follow him into his office, a small room filled with green filing cases. For a fraction of a second María Luisa recalled the sunny day when she and several friends had painted Miss Summer's one green filing case with brilliant red flowers. "It's not half so grim when it's pretty like that," Miss Summer had said. María Luisa thought what fun it would be to paint all the cases in this office. Indeed they did look depressing.

The man was speaking to her, bending over her a little. "I'm Mr. Allen, your counselor. I hear from the secretary that you brought some records with you? Splendid! I'm glad you have them."

He sat down and after a brief intense glance at María

Luisa, he looked through the records Miss Summer had sent. Now and then he made little "h'm" sounds, as though he were thinking very hard.

"Good, very good indeed! Now, María Luisa, tell me about your school. What was it like? Did they speak English or Spanish?"

"It was small, that school. They tell us to speak English so we speak English, but when we forget or can't think of the right word or something like that, the teacher she didn't mind if we speak Spanish. It's what you think that counts."

Mr. Allen nodded his head and looked at her over his glasses. They were very strange glasses that looked as if they had been cut across the middle. "I'm afraid you will find this school very different from the last one you went to. It's a very large school. We try to be one big happy family, but it's not always so easy. Well, we'll let Miss Wall make out a schedule for you . . ."

He seemed on the verge of saying more, but then his telephone rang. He motioned to the secretary who seemed to understand what he wanted. She told María Luisa to sit and wait in her office while she filled out the necessary papers. She telephoned somewhere and asked for Carol to come. Then she made out six filing cards, muttering to herself as she did so. "Where can we put her? Oh, dear, Miss Thompson's class is full. Well, let's see. . . ." María Luisa, perched on the edge of the chair once more felt like an intruder crowding into classes that were already too big. While Miss Wall continued to mutter, a girl came in, a very pretty girl with full pink cheeks and long blond hair that looked as though it had been ironed, it was that smooth.

"Carol, this is María Luisa Santos. This is Carol Kraus. She'll show you to your classes." She handed the class cards to María Luisa who in her confusion mumbled a *gracias* instead of thank you.

"C'mon," Carol said after taking one look at María Luisa. She strode out of the room while María Luisa followed her through the halls, stopping only to point out the obvious places. "This is the Girls' Room; this is the gym. Here's the library. The cafeteria is down the hall, there." Then she looked at María Luisa's class schedule and pointed out the room where her next class would be held. Finally, her duty done, she stopped and stared at María Luisa who had not uttered one word the whole time.

"What are you anyway, a Mexican, a Cuban, or what?" Now the tone of Carol's voice which had been indifferent before was clearly antagonistic.

"I'm an *American*. From Arizona." María Luisa was too surprised to protest. Carol had looked at her with unmistakable hatred. But why?

"You sure look Mexican. You sound it, too," Carol said.

María Luisa could feel the blood mounting to her face and she could have sworn that the little hairs on the back of her neck were raised, which meant she was going to lose her temper. But she was still too amazed to get angry. Perhaps Carol didn't understand.

"My mother was Mexican and so we speak Spanish at home. My father . . ." she was about to explain to Carol that her father had been born in the United States and so he was a citizen, but Carol wasn't interested.

"Brother, this school is something else. Talk about pollution. This really stinks." She spoke too fast and María

Luisa wondered if Carol meant that she smelled. But she had bathed that very morning. "Anyway, I'm not staying around. I'll be going to a private school," Carol finished smugly.

María Luisa had never encountered anything like this before and she hardly knew what to say. Was this the racial prejudice she'd read about and seen on TV? Just then the bell rang, and doors opened and students streamed out of the classrooms into the hall.

"It's like a human river," she thought. She'd never seen anything like it before. They seemed to come in groups, most of them talking loud, some of them fighting: Two boys punched a third who cried out in pain, but nobody intervened; one girl passed a cigarette to another, and a boy and girl walked closely together, kissing each other in a long drawn-out kiss as though there was nobody around to watch them. María Luisa stood open-mouthed. Was this how students behaved in school?

"OK. This is second period. You go to Room 34, down there," Carol had to shout to make herself heard. She pointed vaguely down the hall and disappeared into the crowd.

María Luisa made her way to Room 34, her throat dry, a sure sign that she was afraid. So far school was hardly promising. It was more like a nightmare.

Was this really a class? María Luisa had never been in the middle of so much confusion. Mr. Thompson, the math teacher, a pale gray-haired man in a pale gray suit stood surrounded by students handing him slips of paper which he signed without reading, asking him questions, and making remarks that María Luisa thought extremely rude, but Mr. Thompson seemed not to mind, as though he were used to it. At last he noticed María Luisa, read her schedule slip, and signed it. Everything had to be signed, she noticed. He reached in back of his desk to a bookcase and found a book for María Luisa, pointed out a seat in the back of the room for her, and told her to try to keep up with the class.

At last there was less noise in the class and Mr. Thompson began to teach. At least he was talking but his voice was so soft, María Luisa could hardly hear him, except when he stopped to tell a student to sit down or threatened to send him to the office. Boys flew paper airplanes at each other and two girls near María Luisa were reading comic books. She looked through the math text trying to find the place, but it was hopeless. She hadn't the faintest idea of what they were supposed to be doing.

After class she went up to Mr. Thompson and tried to smile so he wouldn't be angry at her. She cleared her throat and then spoke in a timid voice: "Please, I don' understan'." She shook her head, unable to say any more.

Mr. Thompson scratched his head. "I can't explain it to you right now. I have another class. Try to find out from your classmates what we're doing."

That was hopeless. In San Luis, she had been one of the best students and now it seemed as though she might actually fail in school.

She hurried to the English class, afraid she would not find the room. At any rate, she had always liked English more than math. She found the room just before it was time to close the door. But it turned out that the English class was almost as noisy as the math class had been. The teacher was trying to point out why some sentences in

English were grammatically correct and others incorrect, but to María Luisa they all seemed fine, better than any sentences she had ever written. After a while all the words seemed to run together and then she gave up altogether.

At lunchtime she sat alone in the cafeteria, barely nibbling at the sandwich Aunt Rosa had made for her. Everyone else seemed to have friends. When she looked more carefully, however, she saw several students eating by themselves. One girl stood in the corner and nibbled at an apple, her eyes downcast. Another girl sat alone and dreamed vacantly. María Luisa did not want to know her, for she seemed too fat and dirty; at the same time, she could feel how lonely this poor girl must be because she was just as lonely herself.

"I wonder if they are Mexican, because then maybe we could eat lunch together," she found herself thinking. And then she realized that never before had she stopped to think about what anyone *was*. So Carol Kraus's words had already begun to affect the way she was thinking.

More bells. More classes. From each María Luisa collected a heavy textbook until she had almost more than she could carry. At least one class was promising, Chorus; that day she was too downhearted to sing, but it would be a relief to have music instead of all the talk that was beginning to buzz inside her head.

Now she understood why Mr. Allen had made such a point of asking her how much English she knew. All the teachers talked much too much and far too fast. The steady sound of English hammered on her mind and her ears ached with it.

Maybe Elena and Mike had been right. Maybe school

was a kind of prison from which she could escape when she was eighteen. But she could not wait until then. Besides she had loved school before, but that was all in the past. Tears of disappointment threatened to come but she held them back. And then something happened that was good. In light of everything else that had happened it was almost good enough to be a miracle.

The teacher of her last class, a science class, was a Miss Montez. When María Luisa saw her, she knew instantly that she was a Chicano and that she would understand what María Luisa was going through. As she read the class card that María Luisa offered her, María Luisa felt proud that this teacher should be so nice-looking, a slender young woman, immaculate in a white shirt with a pale blue scarf tucked in neatly at the neck. The familiar black hair was pulled back smoothly and her dark eyes had a warm look about them.

"Her eyes understand mine," María Luisa thought to herself as Miss Montez explained to her briefly and very slowly in English what they were studying. She promised that after class one of the boys would show María Luisa the experiments they were doing so she wouldn't be too far behind.

"We're working on heredity and environment. Do you understand? No? Well, heredity means that you are like your parents and the environment means everything around you that shapes your life. We'll be talking more about it today."

María Luisa breathed a sigh of relief. She understood what Miss Montez had said. With a little hope the first time that day, María Luisa sat down and waited for the class to begin.

Miss Montez might have seemed sympathetic but that didn't mean she was easy. She plunged right into the lecture and discussion, asking questions here and there, drawing diagrams on the board to explain a point, using her hands to describe what she wanted to say. María Luisa did not understand the words, "chromosomes," "genes," "characteristics," and "genetics." These words the rest of the class had had, but Miss Montez, looking at María Luisa, reviewed their meanings so that they were clear. She talked of how children get to resemble their parents and not someone else's, why black cats will have in addition to a black kitten, a gray one or a red one in the litter. All of this was new to María Luisa. For the first time that day she found that she was full of curiosity about something she was supposed to study.

How she admired Miss Montez! She could make the students mind without saying a word. When two boys began to talk, she snapped her fingers and gave them a look that stopped them cold. At the end of the period, she gave the homework assignment. *Caray*, María Luisa thought, this one really gives it to us.

"Aw, Miss Montez," complained a boy, "you give us too much work all the time."

"That's not much at all, Tony. It's not so very hard either. We have a great deal to learn this year."

Everyone groaned, but it wasn't a genuine complaint. It was a way of saving face. Even the kids in San Luis did the same thing when Miss Summer gave them homework.

When María Luisa left the school, her arms aching with a load of books, the fog had gone and the sun had come out. She walked alone although the streets were swarming with students. If it weren't for Miss Montez, she thought, she would be one miserable girl, but Miss Montez had given her the thread of courage that she so sorely needed.

She was splendid, that Miss Montez. And stubborn too; she had not spoken one word of Spanish, although she certainly could have, but she was careful to see that María Luisa understood what she was saying. Now María Luisa began to wonder about her. She began to wonder where she had come from. Mexico? Cuba? South America? It didn't really matter. They were all related.

If only she could go to Miss Montez's class and forget the rest of school! It had been dreadful. But the worst thing of all had been coming up against Carol Kraus. She had heard a lot about prejudice; *caray*, that was no secret. But it had never happened to her before, not directly and mean like this. Even remembering it made her a little sick. She wondered if Miss Montez had ever felt it so directly.

Even if she did, María Luisa reasoned, wasn't one Miss Montez worth more than a hundred Carol Krauses? Of course. This very thought made her feel better and she decided she wouldn't waste any more time thinking about that mean and silly girl.

CHAPTER EIGHT

The minute María Luisa entered the house, she felt something was wrong. This was after school on a Friday, her second week in San Francisco. She was far from happy. Two weeks of school and she was trailing far behind. She managed to keep up in Miss Montez's class, because Miss Montez spoke clearly and slowly enough so that it was easy to understand; besides, María Luisa had never come across anything as fascinating as the science that Miss Montez taught.

But everything else was becoming more and more difficult. Math was hopeless. María Luisa studied each night until Aunt Rosa had to make her turn out the light and go to sleep. Yet she could not seem to catch up with her lessons. She ached from trying to understand English spoken all day long and from trying to fill the gaps that were missing in her schoolwork. Everyday when she walked home, she felt as though her shoulders bent forward a little more than they had the day before under the weight of her books.

"Hello, Luisita," Aunt Rosa called out affectionately that Friday. "How did it go today?"

"Fine," she answered bravely, but without conviction.

Aunt Rosa was always so cheerful. No wonder—she didn't have to go to school. María Luisa almost envied her as she sat in the dining room, a huge pile of dresses on the table in front of her. Instead of going to work in a factory, she stayed at home and did all the handwork on the dresses; sometimes it was embroidery which she did very well indeed, and more often it was hemming, attaching collars and cuffs, and other operations that couldn't be done on a sewing machine.

On that Friday Rosita was crawling around the floor as usual and from Mike's bedroom came the sound of his guitar. He was practicing. Two of Aunt Rosa's neighbors were sitting with her and they, too, were busy sewing and stopping occasionally to sip coffee.

"In the kitchen there is *pan dulce* (sweet roll) for you, and take some milk or some chocolate, María Luisa. You are getting so thin! Much too thin! What will your mother think when she sees you, that I don't feed you?" Then Aunt Rosa added in a low voice, "But first you'd better see Juan. Something is bothering him and he says he won't tell anyone but you."

María Luisa found him sitting in her bedroom on her bed. He looked up at her with eyes full of sadness and as María Luisa put down her books, she felt that her own must be just as sad. From the other room came the sound of the women laughing. And there in the bedroom were the two of them, as sad a brother and sister as could be found anywhere.

She sat beside him and held him close to her for a few

minutes without saying anything. Then she asked, "What's the matter, Juan?"

"I don't like school. I don't like it at all."

"What's wrong with school? Is it the kids you don't like?"

"I don't like the teacher. She's mean and old. She yells all the time and says we are stupid, *burros!* That's the only word she knows. Dumb old teacher, can't even speak Spanish."

Poor Juan! María Luisa knew just how he felt.

"Juanito, you are going to have to learn to speak English. Where we live now, in San Francisco, more people speak English than Spanish. It's not like San Luis, where it's all right to speak Spanish all the time."

"I want to go back there, to San Luis. To Mama and Sister Celeste . . ."

"I know, Juanito. Me, too."

How good it would be to slip down to the bus station, get on the bus and go home! But she was the one who had to be sensible.

"Juan, we don't have a home to go any more. Our house is rented; somebody else lives there now. Besides, Mama is in the hospital and can't take care of us. If we went back, we wouldn't even be able to visit her in the hospital. We'll see her next June—the doctor said so. So we have to stay here. That's all there is to it."

The positive tone she had to take in talking to Juan made her feel more confident now.

"Tell me, Juan. Are you learning to read?"

"We have to learn letters. But I don't understand what that teacher says. She yells."

"That's too bad. But it's not hard to read. Why, I could

teach you that myself. Maybe we can ask the teacher to let you borrow a book, and I'll help you. In Spanish and in English."

She smiled encouragingly as if to say it would be fun. Juan looked doubtful, but less tragic. María Luisa took out her notebook, opened to an empty page and wrote in big letters J U A N.

"There now, what does that say?"

Juan didn't know.

"That's your name, *mi hijito,* my little brother. That says Juan. A 'J'—a 'U'—an 'A'—and an 'N.' J-U-A-N! See if you can write it."

A smile spread over his face. It was good to see his name in letters. He took the paper and pencil from his sister and lay on the floor, tongue sticking out of his mouth in concentration as he copied the letters.

"There," he cried, "I did it! See, María Luisa!"

The letters were long and wobbly, but they spelled out JUAN.

"That's wonderful! Mama will be so happy when you spell out your name for her in a letter. Maybe tomorrow we'll spell Santos."

"But I still don't like school. I don't want to go. You be my teacher."

"I have to go to school myself. And I'm afraid you have to go, too. But if you learn to read and write, then maybe your teacher won't yell so much. I can teach you a little bit every day."

He looked more hopeful. He wiped his nose on his sleeve, as though he were through with tears and sniffling for a while.

"And today it's Friday. Time to play. Want to go out?"

He kissed her on the cheek, a shy little-boy kiss, and when María Luisa went down to the street five minutes later, he was as noisy and spirited as any of his friends.

Some girls were playing jump rope. Children. They didn't even go to Junior High School yet. María Luisa watched them wistfully and then asked, "Can I play, too?"

In a minute she was jumping rope, doing "Rosie, Rosie!" and "Red Hot Pepper!" The color came back into her cheeks and she forgot all about school, all about San Luis, and all about growing up.

If only she could, she would be a child for the rest of her life!

CHAPTER NINE

"María Lu-EES-a!"

Aunt Rosa leaned out of the window and called her niece in a loud musical voice. Even the children in the street who were used to their mother's calling them in a way that was not much different, invariably smiled and imitated Aunt Rosa.

It hadn't been hard for Aunt Rosa to get María Luisa to play with the younger girls who lived on the block. "You study, study, study too much, all the time, María Luisa. It's crazy, all that studying. Makes you pale and thin. You're still a little girl. Go play a little. I'll call you when dinner's ready."

One clear late afternoon in October when Aunt Rosa called her in for dinner, María Luisa regretfully took off the roller skates a little friend had let her borrow. Running up the stairs she stopped briefly to listen to Mike playing his guitar, the classical one, not the electric. He had confessed he wanted to learn classical guitar, even though he might never play it in public. It was plenty hard, he said, but very beautiful. The music kept singing in María Luisa's ears even as she washed and helped Elena set the table. Dinner was ready and it was time to sit down.

"Where's Juan?"

"I don't know. I haven't seen him."

Aunt Rosa went to the window and called him in her clear contralto voice. But he didn't come.

"Maybe he's playing on the next block," María Luisa suggested. "I'll go get him. I'll only take a minute."

On the next street his friend, Manuel, was playing with a ball. "Hey, Manuel, did you see my brother, Juan?"

He shook his head no.

Perhaps he had gone to the grocery store for candy. *Abuelita* was forever spoiling him, giving him pennies and nickels. But the man at the grocery store hadn't seen him.

María Luisa did not dare confess to herself that now she was getting worried. Every day now she and Juan had had lessons in reading and writing, and he was doing very well. María Luisa always made it seem like a game, he had said. Yet he still came home from school in tears.

When María Luisa walked back to the house, Aunt Rosa had already begun to serve the soup and was surprised when Juan wasn't with his sister. Grasping at any straw now, María Luisa looked under the table and then in all the closets to see if he was hiding. She looked in all the bedrooms; he might have fallen asleep. No, he wasn't there either.

Had he gone off with friends? Had he even come home from school? Roberto said he had, but then he had told Roberto he was going away for a while. Roberto thought he had gone to play with Manuel.

Panic sent prickles up and down María Luisa's spine. Juan lost in the city, this enormous city! *Dios mío*, how would they ever find him? Where would they look? Where could he be?

He was such a little boy. Only six years old. A little boy with sober dark eyes.

Everyone had a solution. He was still in the schoolyard. He was on the swings at Golden Gate Park. He was at a friend's house. He had been kidnapped and held for ransom. He went for a walk across the Golden Gate Bridge.

As if those suggestions were not awful enough, worse ones pictured themselves in María Luisa's mind: Juan crossing the street and getting crushed by a big bus. Juan falling from the top of a building. Juan beaten up by thugs. How would she ever be able to tell her mother?

All at once she was laughing and crying and could not seem to stop.

"Cut that out this minute," Mike spoke sternly and shook her narrow shoulders hard; it brought her to her senses. His intense eyes held hers and now he spoke more gently. "You're worried, of course, but what you have to do now is think and not get all worked up."

"Look at this city, Mike! It's so big. Anything could happen to him, anything. And he's such a little boy!"

"All right. He's a little boy, but he's not a stupid little boy. María Luisa, think!"

"Well, it's not the grocery store, and it's not the kids on the next block. It can't be the schoolyard because he hates school. . . ."

With that last consideration, the answer came to María Luisa so clear and simple that she knew it had to be right. Of course he hated school. The lessons that María Luisa gave him helped considerably so that he was not falling behind. Still, the teacher yelled at him and the kids in the playground, even the Chicano kids, made fun of him. No amount of reason from María Luisa could make him change his mind about going home.

"I'll bet he's at the bus station. I bet anything that's where he is. More than anything else, he wants to go back to San Luis," María Luisa said.

"Poor little boy," Aunt Rosa said, her face wearing a look of disappointment. "Is he so unhappy here with us?"

"Of course not. It's not you, Aunt Rosa, or anyone here. He loves you all. It's the school."

"C'mon, María Luisa. Let's go right away and see. You may be right," Mike said, getting up from the table.

They ran down the street, caught the bus and rode over to the Greyhound Terminal. This was no place for a small boy. The station was crowded and María Luisa had the same sinking sensation she had the very first day when she had had to look for Aunt Rosa there. This was even worse, for Aunt Rosa had been looking for her niece, but Juan was not expecting his sister to come after him, that is, if he was there.

Mike and María Luisa walked all through the station and did not see him. They felt their hopes rise suddenly when they saw a small boy emerging from the Men's Room. From the back it looked like Juan, but when they rushed over, they found it was another little boy. The two cousins looked at each other helplessly.

"I guess I was wrong."

The loudspeaker announced that a bus was departing from Track Three.

"Wait a minute," Mike cried, "he might be out there trying to get on."

He grabbed María Luisa's hand and led her through the crowds to the place where the buses were lined up. Sure enough, there, leaning against a wall, looking fascinated and frightened at the same time, was Juan, whole and unharmed. María Luisa rushed over to him, put her arms around him and kissed him over and over again. Then he really did look bewildered.

"Juan, what on earth are you doing here? You had us all so worried. What are you doing here?"

"I'm going home, María Luisa," he spoke calmly, as though that should be obvious enough. "Can you tell me which bus to take? I have fifty cents. See?"

"*Idiota, imbécil.* . . . oh, my little darling!" Relieved to find him, María Luisa began to scold him, to kiss him again, to shake him, to hug him, all at once.

"You can't go home, Juan. I told you that. We have to stay here until June anyway."

Tears moistened his eyes. "I won't go to school any more."

Mike took his hand and led him into the station. He sat down and held Juan on his lap.

"Listen, Juan, I can't do much about your teacher. But I'm going to teach you to fight so you don't get beat up. It's one of those things you have to learn. There comes a time when you can't run home to your mama. You have to learn to punch the other guy in the nose. I'm going to teach you how to do it. Then the kids'll be afraid to beat you up." He nodded and winked at Juan, as if to show this would be their secret.

"How do you know all this?"

"How do I know? Because once I was a little boy. I had to learn to fight so that the other kids wouldn't beat me up. It's not so hard. Anyway, you can't go home because I want to take you fishing. Did you know there are places in San Francisco where you can go fishing? I'll bet you didn't, did you?"

"Would you take me fishing?"

"Sure, but we gotta go home right now because Aunt Rosa is waiting for us. Stay here with your sister for a minute. I'll be right back."

He went over to the candy counter and came back with three chocolate bars. "Don't tell your Aunt Rosa that we're going to have these before dinner."

"OK," Juan said, as he brightened considerably.

María Luisa picked up the brown paper bag in which Juan had packed his pajamas as he was about to leave them behind. Then they all took the bus back home.

"Mike, I thank you so much. You are a wonderful person, just wonderful," María Luisa said. "Juan is crazy about you. I can tell."

"Well, I like him, too. It can't be easy, not having a father and your mother in the hospital. Maybe a big brother will help a little."

"A girl can use a big brother, too," she said. Mike touched her hand and then the two of them bent over to listen to Juan who was already spinning out a colorful account of his escapade. He added his own flourishes, how he was chased by a squadron of cops, how he fought a gang single-handed, and how he had run to the bus station from Fourteenth Street in less than ten minutes.

"Yeah?" Mike asked, and then he whispered to María Luisa. "That kid brother of yours has a talent, did you know that?"

CHAPTER TEN

It was a Saturday night in November. Everyone was going out excepting the little boys who had been at a party that afternoon and were busy blowing party horns at each other. Uncle Emilio was working. Mike was playing at the Club and María Luisa had offered to baby-sit so that Aunt Rosa could go to a baby shower. Even *Abuelita* had gone out to visit her friends and at the moment Elena was getting dressed to go out with her friend, Connie.

María Luisa sat in front of Grandmother's trunk which she used as a desk. She had intended to use the quiet evening in another attack on math. She could not fail, not only because it would make Miss Summer and Sister Celeste feel bad but she herself could never stand the disgrace of it. It would have to work through sheer persistence, if nothing else.

But she found herself staring at Elena who stood in front of the mirror trying on one necklace and then another. Connie, holding a transistor radio close to her ear, hummed and rolled her heavy hips to the rock 'n' roll rhythm while a singer pleaded, "C'mon, baby, c'mon, c'mon!" A fat ugly girl whose black hair puffed up in a ridiculous mass of curls, she made Elena more beautiful than ever by contrast.

Elena caught María Luisa's glance in the mirror. The mischievous gleam grew in Elena's eye and María Luisa knew that she was about to be teased and made to look ridiculous in front of Connie. Someday she would have the sense to walk out of the room when she saw that look in Elena's eyes, but at the moment she remained helpless, a bird hypnotized by a snake.

"Look at the saint, Connie. María Luisa. She's an intellectual, did you know? She wouldn't dream of looking at a boy, not if there's a book around," she said contemptuously.

Connie made a grimace, one finger in a mouth that wore an idiot smile and crossed eyes looking upward as though she were a demented angel. Elena burst into peals of laughter.

Vexed, María Luisa decided to attack Connie. If she was looking for a fight, she would get it. "Hey, Connie, you're busting out of your dress in back."

Connie turned to see if it were so and Elena laughed. It wasn't quite true, but it might have been. Connie had large rolls of fat and the seams of her dresses were frequently strained. It was a worry María Luisa would never have.

"Shut up, *imbécil!*" Connie said.

"Actually, you don't know our little cousin," Elena went on. "She only pretends to study. The minute we leave, about twenty boy friends come up. She's one popular girl. Wow!"

"I'll bet," Connie giggled as she turned up the radio to full volume. María Luisa pretended to read, not wanting the girls to see that Elena's teasing hurt her feelings. She wished they would hurry and then leave her alone. It took Elena forever to put on her makeup. First the base, then the blush, more eye-shadow, liner, eyebrows, powder, practically half a bottle of perfume, and earrings almost four inches long. Elena put a jeweled butterfly in her black hair, took it out, considered a velvet ribbon, and then put the butterfly on once more, smiling as she adjusted the ornament. How nice it would be to be so pleased with yourself, María Luisa thought, a little enviously.

At last they were ready to leave. "Don't read all your books tonight. Save some for tomorrow," Elena said, and then smiling at Connie as though she had said something witty, she left the house.

María Luisa lay on the bed, her head resting on *Abuelita's* old serape and she looked into space, seeing nothing.

Would she ever understand Elena? Mike said that teasing people made her feel superior. One moment she could be mean, stinging like a wasp, but if María Luisa burst into tears then she would be all apologies, apologies that sounded as though she really meant them. She would put her arms around her cousin and swear she was only having fun and María Luisa mustn't take her so seriously.

"Well, I'm not going to burst into tears just to make her feel better every time," María Luisa said out loud even though there was nobody there to hear her.

The trouble was that Elena could be so kind. She had spent several hours making over her discarded dresses so that they would fit her cousin. Nothing came of it; they never looked right and in the end they went back into the closet. It was too bad, but it did not really matter. Elena had been so interested. Several times, too, she had invited María Luisa to go with her while she shopped for a new dress or a pair of shoes. María Luisa had been thrilled to be with her cousin and each time she had thought that now they were really friends, only to have Elena attack her again when she least expected it.

Well, Mike had warned her that she was a jealous person. It was what Elena herself had said that bothered María Luisa. Elena had looked into her eyes and remarked, not once but several times, very thoughtfully, "You're different, María Luisa. I don't know what it is about you, but you're different.

One of the girls who now sometimes ate with María Luisa in the lunchroom had said the same thing one day. "I don't know exactly why, but you sure are different. You're not like the rest of us." The next day the girl had sat at a different table.

Am I really different? How? In what way? What a fail-ure I am, a failure in every way, she thought.

She looked down on the city below. The lights seemed un-usually bright and one red neon sign in particular kept flash-ing on and off as though it were saying *Come, come, come, come, come!*

Come where? Do what? Brimming over in self-pity, María Luisa looked in Elena's mirror and made a face at the miserable girl she saw there. How pale she was! Maybe a little color . . .

She picked up Elena's rouge brush and rubbed some color over her cheeks. There, that was so much better, and if that helped . . .

Impulsively, she took off her blouse and put a towel over her shoulders as she had seen Elena do before making up her face. Blush, eye-shadow, liner over and under the lids. It really made a difference. It wasn't so easy to put on mas-cara but it made her eyes larger than ever. The lipstick smeared at first, so she took it off and tried again. She looked at herself in the mirror. Not bad at all. Why, she didn't hate herself after all!

Hair? She pulled out the elastic that held it together in back and let it fall. She took Elena's brush and began to brush it vigorously as she had seen Elena do. It seemed to come to life, taking on the slightly blue sheen that her cousin's hair had, and when she let her hair hang loosely over her shoulders she did not look so much like a prim and prissy child.

In the closet she found a daring blue dress, one that looked enchanting on Elena. Oh, dear, it was too big! She found some pins in Aunt Rosa's room and pinned the hem up high above her knees, about as short as Elena's dresses. But what should she do about the two puffs of material in front which Elena filled out so nicely but which hung loosely over María Luisa's breasts which were only beginning to round? She ran to the other room, found some newspaper which she crumpled up and shoved in front of her dress. It was a little bumpy and it rattled, but it was better than being flat like a very little girl.

Now for the stockings, the shiny black party shoes, and a generous spray of perfume. María Luisa looked in the mirror. Like Cinderella, she had become dazzling. Where was the coach, the footman, even someone on a Honda? She was ready to go out, but where and with whom?

Well, she would go out anyway. She put on an old cape of Elena's and went downstairs to sit on the porch. The houses along the street seemed full of light, as though everyone were having a party. Late as it was, children were still playing in the street. A couple clinging close to one another strolled down the street and she overheard fragments of Spanish. "You are so sweet. So sweet. I adore you. I love . . ."

She sat on the porch all alone and soon it grew cold. She thought she heard Rosita cry and hurried upstairs but Rosita was sleeping innocently in her crib. María Luisa took off the cape and the dress, the lovely black shoes and the stockings and put them all away. She wiped away the makeup and washed her face. Then, putting on her plain white nightgown, crawled into bed.

She wondered if anyone else in all that city was as lonely as she!

CHAPTER ELEVEN

María Luisa had learned one thing. Nothing stays gloomy forever. Before November was out, she had a birthday, her thirteenth. And a surprise party to celebrate it!

Aunt Rosa had bought a cake with pink and green roses sculptured in the icing and thirteen blazing candles. Then everyone brought out gifts for María Luisa. Pantyhose from Elena, a suede purse from Mike, carefully wrapped bubble gum from the little boys, a pair of very old silver earrings from *Abuelita* who said she had had them since she was a little girl, and then, after a lengthy speech from Uncle Emilio about María Luisa's excellent qualities and how she was like a daughter to him and to Aunt Rosa, he handed her an envelope in which was tucked twenty dollars. With Aunt Rosa's help and advice, she was to buy herself some new clothes. A miracle! So many presents and so much money all at once made her eyes shine. She wanted to kiss everyone.

The very next day María Luisa and Aunt Rosa went shopping on Market Street and came home with what María

Luisa had wanted for a long time now. A red plaid skirt with a leather belt, a turtleneck sweater, new shoes, and red tights. Some of the girls at school noticed and chirped, "How darling!" the next day when María Luisa wore her new outfit to school, and María Luisa thought that a few of the boys were looking at her all through the day. She was a poor relation no longer, but María Luisa Santos, an individual. Thinking so made everything easier. For three perfect days, she lived on a spree of happiness. When she came home on the fourth day, it was all over.

Aunt Rosa had looked at her sadly when she came in from school.

"What's the matter?" she asked. Bad news from her mother?

Aunt Rosa gave her the letter that had come from the school. María Luisa was failing in everything but science where she barely passed the course, and in Chorus, which didn't matter anyway.

She tried to smile and pretend it didn't matter, because Juan was standing right there looking at her. But the tears spilled over. She locked herself in the bathroom and cried for a long time. But she couldn't stay there forever, so she went to her room where she sat alone, staring straight ahead. What made it worse was that everybody knew. Juan waited silently in the hall.

"Don't take it so hard," Elena said. "Lots of kids get letters like that. I got one once. They'll pass you anyway, even if you flunk, because they don't want to keep you in school forever. Anyway, what's a mark? A little pen scrawl on a card, that's all."

But it did mean something to María Luisa. Perhaps Miss Summer had been old-fashioned when she had said that if you let yourself fail once, then it was easy to let yourself fail again and pretty soon failing would be a habit.

"I don't like being dumb," María Luisa had cried. In San Luis she had been bright without half trying.

It was all too confusing. Some of the things María Luisa had to learn didn't make sense at all and it seemed silly to work so hard to understand them. Math was ridiculous, full of A's, B's, and X, Y, Z's which were always getting into puzzling situations. What use was that? In English she had to learn rules and rules and rules, and long involved words like "predicate nominative" and "dangling participles" which she didn't quite understand. Even if she memorized all the rules of grammar, she still did not understand English when the teachers spoke it so fast and she had to hear it all day long until her ears rang.

Besides, no matter what Elena said, marks did mean something. If she got very good marks, Miss Summer had said, she might even be able to go to college.

"And you should go, María Luisa. You're a bright girl!" she had said.

A bright girl? That was a big joke now. Maybe Carol Kraus had been right when she looked down on her. Maybe she really was stupid and worthless.

She lay on her bed and dreamed of San Luis. Each year the class put on a festival with both Spanish and American folksongs and dances. "This is what you have inherited, all of you, and you can be proud of it," Miss Summer had said. No child in that school had ever cried because a teacher called him stupid. San Luis had been a heaven, like the childhood she left there, but only now was she beginning to understand that.

She was glad that Miss Summer could not see her now. She was becoming what Miss Summer used to call a "klunkhead," one of those students who sit and say nothing all day long. Once in class María Luisa had volunteered to answer a question, but without realizing what she was doing, changed from English to Spanish in the middle of a sentence. A few kids laughed and she never volunteered again.

It was Uncle Emilio's night off and when he came to dinner with the family, María Luisa was more ashamed than ever of her red eyes. She sat through dinner silently while everyone else politely made conversation about other things, for they understood how she felt. After dinner, as she dried the dishes, Aunt Rosa said, "You mustn't worry so. Do you think we would beat you if you got a bad report card? Of course not. You're a fine girl and all of us love you. That is the truth!"

Even Uncle Emilio had kind words for her. He watched her as she dried the dishes. Then he pulled out a kitchen chair and told her to sit down because he wanted to talk to her. Even if his words hardly comforted her, the gentleness of his voice did. It was like having a father.

"Tell me, Luisita, who likes a girl who can do mathematics, a girl who reads books? That means nothing. That's not what a girl is for. A girl should be beautiful. She should smile and laugh a lot and even sing a little. You don't need math for that or all this studying. Do you know what school is? It's a place where you go until you are old enough to get married. Then you become a woman. First you are a nice wife, a good cook and housekeeper; later you have beautiful babies. Nothing in the world is more beautiful than to be a mother. So don't worry about school."

Aunt Rosa, holding a chubby Rosita in her arms, had something to add. "María Luisa, let me tell you, life is the best teacher of all. Believe me, I have lived a long time and I know. Life itself will teach you all you need to know, and some things you don't even want to know. School is all right, like Uncle Emilio says, but it's not the only place where you learn."

They made it so easy for María Luisa to give up. They were so good, trying to make her feel better. Impulsively she kissed them.

Still, when she went to bed that night, she could not believe that school was not important and that Miss Summer had been mistaken in expecting her to do well.

The letter had to be signed and returned to school. Uncle Emilio's signature was big and flourishing. Anyone would think he was proud of his niece, María Luisa thought bitterly. She gave the letter to the secretary in the office the next day and her cheeks burned with shame.

CHAPTER TWELVE

The English class was interrupted by a girl acting as office messenger as she handed the teacher a note. The teacher looked up. "María Luisa Santos, you're to go to the office at once."

What could it be? Frightened, María Luisa hurried to the office. Had she done something wrong or could it be a disturbing message from home? She sat on the edge of a chair in the waiting room along with two boys who were obviously in some sort of trouble and a pathetic little girl who looked as though she would never smile again. A large girl with plastic-looking hair sat vacantly and chewed gum.

"Maybe I'm a misfit, too," María Luisa thought.

A serious-looking lady with large round glasses called out her name and María Luisa followed her into a small room. The lady told her to sit down at the table where a boy with long straight blond hair was already sitting. He grinned at María Luisa openly.

"You needn't be so frightened," the lady said, "we're

only going to take a few tests. You might even enjoy them. Just do what you can. Read the directions. Well, maybe we'd better read them together. Then we can begin. Remember, it doesn't matter if you can't finish."

They were certainly odd tests, but in a way they were fun, like puzzles. Some of María Luisa's were in Spanish and the blond boy had his in a language María Luisa didn't understand. They weren't allowed to talk, but they smiled at each other and sometimes the boy would say, "Phew" at the end of the test, as though it had been hard. During the course of the morning, María Luisa heard the lady speak the boy's name. It was Peter Jensen.

The morning seemed to fly. The bell rang, the tests were over and it was already time for lunch. María Luisa was bewildered. What were these tests all about?

Two days later the counselor, Mr. Allen, called María Luisa to the office. She waited while he talked on the telephone. What an odd man he was, she thought, with a smile he could wipe on or off as he pleased. He began with a smile but wiped it off in favor of a serious look, as though he were sympathizing with her about something. Then he cleared his throat.

"Well, María Luisa. Tell me, now that you've been in school for some time, what do you think of it?"

Should she tell him the truth, that the little school in San Luis was a hundred times better? He might feel hurt. It was better to go slow.

"It's very big this school, and there are many people here."

"H'mmmmmm," he sounded as though he were thinking serious thoughts. "Speak up now so I can hear you. Do you speak Spanish at home?"

"Yes, sir. My cousin sometime she speak English with me and I teach my little brother English. Every day."

"Very good. Do you find it easy to understand the English that is spoken in class?"

"Sometime, Mr. Allen. Not too much. They go so fast. It's too much English. I try to understan' but I get tired and then it's just sounds."

"H'mmm, I can well imagine. María Luisa, you know you're a bright girl. If it weren't for the language problem . . ." at that point the telephone rang and once more María Luisa had to sit and wait while he talked of something else. At last he put down the receiver.

"There's going to be a special class in English every day after school. Actually it's an experiment. It will last a few months. Maybe it will work, maybe not. Now then, you don't have to take it unless you want to. There won't be any grades or any credit, and you'll still have to keep up with your other classes just the same. But it might help. What do you think?"

If he had told her that standing on her head an hour a day would help, she would have been glad to do so.

"Please, Mr. Allen, I would like very much."

"All right, but don't be too hopeful now. These things come and go. Experiments. Some of them are a waste if ever I saw it, but now and then one works out. You can try."

The telephone rang again, and as Mr. Allen talked, he filled out the necessary forms for María Luisa with instructions about the time and place for the experimental class.

He was not as encouraging as he might have been. Perhaps he did not really believe it would work. María Luisa looked at the paper, however, as though it held a promise. These days she felt as though she were at the bottom of a deep well and the only way she could look was up.

CHAPTER THIRTEEN

Monday was a difficult day and after school, when María Luisa went to the sewing room where the special class was to be held, it seemed useless to imagine that she would ever learn English well enough to keep up with her classes. As for the stories she once felt that she wanted to write, why even think about them, she asked herself.

Ten students had already arrived and were waiting for the class to begin. Each sat quietly at the sewing tables, lost in a gloomy world of his own. The only sounds came from two little Japanese girls who sat close together, whispering and giggling softly as though they were telling secrets. They reminded María Luisa of little birds.

Sitting at the back of the room, María Luisa recognized several students she had seen before. Julien Alvarez, a tall dark-skinned boy from her science class, sat scratching his initials on the table with a penknife. There was Steve Ramos, a short boy with large luminous eyes. And Gloria Sanchez.

At the sight of Gloria, María Luisa felt a slight flush of guilt. Gloria, one of the most miserable creatures María Luisa had ever seen, was the fat girl with the snarled black hair who always sat alone in the cafeteria. Once María Luisa had asked the two girls with whom she sometimes ate lunch if they wouldn't invite Gloria to eat with them. "To make her feel good, you know?" María Luisa had said. Each of the girls knew what it was like to be alone and have no friends, and yet they had turned up their noses. "Her? Oh, no, she smells!" María Luisa had continued to sit with her friends and pretend to herself that she did not see Gloria sitting by herself every day.

Now everyone sat together at the sewing tables, but each of them was alone. "We're all klunkheads," María Luisa decided. It was easy to be a klunkhead, but dull. One simply never talked, that was all there was to it. Then one couldn't be laughed at. But it could become boring.

A sound of whistling broke the silence and Peter Jensen strode into the room with all the assurance in the world. He was no klunkhead, that was certain. Sitting down and slouching in an exaggerated way, he looked around openly at the others in the class. He whistled continuously, now imitating bird sounds, as though he was determined to make the others snap out of their gloom. María Luisa didn't mean to stare, but she could not help it; he was so different from the boys she had always known, with his rangy long body, his shock of straight blond hair, and the nose that seemed to jut forward;

Miss Summer had told her once that that kind of nose was a sign of curiosity. Peter felt her glance and turned around to stare at her, which embarrassed her dreadfully and made her pretend to be searching for something in her purse. One by one, everyone turned to grin at Peter, while he nodded and grinned in return. "He's the *only* one who isn't a klunkhead," María Luisa thought.

The teacher was almost ten minutes late and there was the question of whether or not she would come. "We don't have to stay," one of the boys said and he had even started toward the door when the teacher walked in.

Or was it the teacher, María Luisa wondered? She looked more like a high school student. She wasn't remarkably pretty, not like Elena; María Luisa found herself comparing everyone to Elena these days. But there was something beautiful about this teacher, something more than the dark curly hair and the direct blue eyes. Her face was flushed with hurrying and now everyone was staring at her.

"I'm late and I'm really very sorry. I didn't mean to keep you waiting. There was a traffic jam on the freeway and everyone was held up. I just couldn't get through."

Someone in the class should have said that was all right, or good afternoon, or we're glad you came, but nobody said a word. Everyone stared. When she spoke, she did not seem like a teacher but more like a person beginning a conversation. Finally Peter responded.

"Is OK. Ve didn't mind waiting."

It was the first time María Luisa had heard him speak. The words were all right but his accent was so thick, María Luisa could barely understand what he said.

The teacher rewarded him with a sparkling smile. She wasn't really pretty, María Luisa decided, but she could not take her eyes away from her. Without knowing why, she had begun to feel better since the teacher came.

"It's very formal in here, isn't it, everyone sitting in rows. Do you suppose we could put four of these big tables together and then when we sit around them, we'll be able to talk with each other," the teacher said.

Three of the boys moved quickly to do this and soon the students and the teacher were sitting around the tables. It was no longer an ordinary class facing one foe, the teacher. It was a group and the teacher was one part of it. Finally they were ready to begin. All eyes were on the new teacher. "*Caray*, I like that pink dress she's wearing and that silk scarf around her neck. I'll have to remember to tell Elena about it," María Luisa thought. Then the teacher began to speak.

"My name is Miss Stein. As you may have been told, this is an experimental class and it's voluntary. That means you don't have to take it if you don't want to. However, if you do take it, it will be important for you to come every day. Any questions?"

"This is an English class, no?" someone asked.

"In a way it is, but I wouldn't want to call it that because it's not like the usual English classes you go to. I like to think of this as a time when we can talk to one another and listen to each other. We'll be talking in English, so that we begin to feel at home with it. It's like learning a musical instrument, you know; the more you practice the better you become. Does anyone else have a question? It's all right to talk out, you know."

Silence from the klunkheads. They might be free to talk out but the habit of keeping still was strong. Finally Peter asked a question.

"Miss Stein, why do they call this class 'experiment'?"

It was difficult to understand him. He spoke English but it seemed to be coming through layers of cheesecloth. Even Miss Stein looked at him kindly but questioningly, as though she hadn't really heard him.

"Hey, teacher, I can't understan' him. Why don't he talk English?" Alex asked.

"I speak English," Peter insisted, but his face turned red.

"Wow, he sure have a accent," Alex said. Everyone smiled. If anyone had an accent it was Alex himself, but he was easy to understand for he seemed to speak a language that lay halfway between English and Spanish. Someone began to josh him in a soft Spanish voice, but Miss Stein saved the day.

"I think the question is, why is this an experimental class and why were you all chosen for it. A good question. You were selected very carefully; you are all capable of doing good work in school, but if you were able to speak and use English better, you would do much better than you seem to be doing now. The experiment is to help you feel easier with the English language."

It was good to be chosen. So perhaps somebody did care, María Luisa thought. But Alex looked doubtful. Miss Stein turned to him.

"You look as though you wanted to say something?"

Alex thought for a minute, shook his head no and looked down at his desk, a klunkhead once more.

"All right then. I think we should get acquainted with each other. Let's go around the table and you may introduce yourselves."

One after the other the names were spoken.

Alex Alvarez

Ralph Covarrubias
Charlie Sun
John García
Steve Muñoz
Tassos Pappas
Riko Takahashi
Ruth Kimura
Paul Ramos
María Luisa Santos
Jesús Hidalgo
Peter Jensen
Gloria Sanchez

The voices were sometimes high in pitch and sometimes so low they were barely audible. Still, there was something rhythmical about the sound of the names, almost musical, María Luisa thought. Could you make a poem out of names, she wondered.

"Now we know each other. We'll get to know each other even more as time goes on. Let's see, do we have time to write today? We'll be writing every day, of course." She looked at her watch doubtfully, not realizing what the prospect of writing every day meant to the class. Students looked at each other and made faces. Who wanted to write?

"You don't mean we're goin' to write *every day*?" Alex asked, hardly able to believe it.

"Why not?" Miss Stein answered with a comforting smile. "Don't look so frightened. Writing is only a way of saying what you think. Actually we'll spend most of the time talking but we'll write, too."

"She'd never get away with it if she weren't so pretty," Alex mumbled in Spanish to Steve. Everyone understood who knew Spanish. But it was Miss Stein who answered the remark, in perfectly clear Spanish. Translated, her answer was:

"Don't knock it until you try it. It will be better than you think."

"You speak Spanish, Miss Stein? You a Chicano?"

"Naw, she from Cuba, I bet."

Miss Stein said, "I'll let you figure it out for yourselves. We don't have time to write now, but we'll do it tomorrow. Don't anyone worry about it. I promise I'll leave work earlier so that I can get here on time. So, I'll see you tomorrow. Good night, now."

María Luisa, walking home, hardly noticed the weight of her books. Her mind was full of new thoughts, all about Miss Stein. She would see her again tomorrow. Now she had something to look forward to.

As she walked up the hill she heard a whistle and saw that Peter Jensen was walking on the other side of the street. He waved to her and she nodded a shy hello. She would be seeing him the next day, too. Smiling to herself, she hurried home.

CHAPTER FOURTEEN

The next day Miss Stein was waiting for them. She had placed a large bag full of apples in the middle of the tables.

"Help yourselves," she said. "You must get awfully hungry at this time of day."

Nobody made a move to take an apple, so she repeated her offer. "Go ahead. Don't be shy." María Luisa hoped someone would take one; otherwise Miss Stein might be hurt, but she herself was too shy to begin. Peter was the first who took an apple and offered it to Ruth Kimura who giggled as she accepted it. Soon everyone was eating apples and talking a little, that is everyone excepting John García, an extremely thin, dark boy who had not as yet said a single word.

"Won't you have one?" Miss Stein asked.

He shook his head, no.

"He don't never eat lunch," Ralph said.

"No? Why not?" Miss Stein's voice was sympathetic, but when John seemed to sink down in his seat, she went on to talk about something else. The other students knew why John hadn't had lunch; there were free lunches for all students who couldn't afford to pay, but John was too proud to ask for the free ticket.

Following an impulse, María Luisa took an apple and gave it to him. He looked at it for a minute, and then took it.

Miss Stein was talking. "I'd like to get to know you all better. We can talk for a while if you like, and then we'll write. Call it what you like; the subject is WHO I AM." She wrote it on the blackboard in large open letters.

"Hey, miss, can we write in Spanish?"

"Let's try it in English first. All right?"

"*Caray,* who I am!" María Luisa asked herself. "I'm María Luisa Santos. I'm me, myself. So what is there to write?" Apparently everyone else was puzzled, too. They looked questioningly at Miss Stein.

"Hey, Teacher. I don' wanna write about who I am. Can I write about my brother? He's got lots to write about." It was Steve Muñoz who asked, almost in a whisper. He looked too young for the class and Miss Stein wondered if he had been pushed ahead by accident. He looked as if he should be in the fifth or sixth grades, not Junior High School.

"I'd rather know about you, Steve."

"But my brother, he's in the Marines."

"I don't know how to say nothin', Miss Stein."

"Please, Miss Stein, can't I write it in Spanish? You understan' Spanish. You speak it good, Miss Stein."

Peter was already scribbling away on a large yellow pad. Charlie Sun had begun to write very slowly and neatly on a page from a notebook. Jesús Hidalgo, an extremely handsome young man who looked as if he might be in high school, had also chewed on his pencil thoughtfully and then began to write. Everyone else looked doubtful. How did one start?

"Let's think of it this way," Miss Stein said. "Everyone of you is an individual and each one of you is different from everybody else. Right?" The class nodded in agreement. "You can write about the things which make you different, if you like; perhaps it's where you were born and where you have traveled. Or maybe you have ideas which seem to be *your* ideas. Perhaps there are things that you really love doing. All of these things help make up your own personality. The best way to start is to start and let the ideas begin to flow without worrying. I'm not going to show these papers to anyone, you know; they are confidential. So you can feel free to say whatever you like."

María Luisa usually had more ideas about what she would like to write than she could ever have time for. Now she could not think of anything to say. Besides, there were so many people sitting around her, tapping the tables with their pens and making noises as they tried to think of what to say, she could almost feel their confusion.

"Miss Stein," she asked with a boldness that surprised her, "would it be all right if I sat in the corner? If I write, I like to be alone."

"Of course, sit wherever you are most comfortable. You can move around."

In the corner, away from the others, María Luisa felt a little wall of quiet around her and then she began to write. She concentrated so hard that she frowned a little and bit her tongue. The room had become very quiet and she could hear the clock on the wall loudly ticking.

who I AM
MARÍA Luisa SANTOS

I AM MARÍA Luisa SANTOS AND I AM AMERICAN.
My FAther he WAS AMERICAN to. HE WAS FROM
TEXAS AND MY MOTHER she is FROM MEXICO. I
AM born IN AirZONA. IN our house WE SPEK
SPANISH AND the church it is IN SPANISH to
AND IN shcoL the ticher MISS SUMMER
Let us SPEK SPANISH WEN WE Like.
IT WAS VERY good thAt schoL ANd the
ticher WANT us to be hAPPY AND NOT Like
herE.

WHEN MY FAther WAS Living he woud
PLAY gitAR SOMETiME ANd be good but
WHEN he got dronk he WAS bAd and
beet MY MOTHER AND ME. ONE day his
truck turN OVER AND WAS KiLL. My
MOTHER is IN host hospitL Now she
has teebee. My Little boTHER AND
I are IN SAN PrANCisco wit MY AuNt
AND uncL.
IN SAN Luis WAS NOT ALL good but
SINCE I AM herE I KNow MORE how
it WAS good thERE. I WAS chiLd theN,
A Little griL. Now I AM growing up.
is big hERE iN SAN FrANCisco but is
NOT So hAPPy.

She read over the paper she had written. She sighed. It wasn't really very good. She had crossed out words and wasn't sure about spelling. Anyway, now Miss Stein would know she was a citizen; after her experience with Carol, that seemed very important indeed.

"Here is my story. It's not very good," she apologized as she gave her paper to Miss Stein.

"Don't worry. It's probably better than you think. Anyway, I'm sure you're going to improve."

María Luisa noticed that some of the members of the class had written papers with only one sentence, and Steve Muñoz had written nothing at all.

One by one the students left the sewing room and nobody spoke very much. "We are all so used to being alone," María Luisa thought, "that we can't get used to saying things like hello and good-bye."

A thick San Francisco fog had been brewing all day and it was chilly. Perhaps the theme she had written hadn't been very good, and she knew of at least two words she had spelled wrong. Now that the time for writing was over she began to think of all the things she might have said and wished Miss Stein would let them write the theme over the next day. It would be so much better then.

"Hey, wait a minute, María Luisa! Gosh, you walk fast."

She barely understood what he said, but she knew that Peter was running to catch up to her. "I only went to get a book and when I turn back around you were gone," he said.

They walked along the street together. "So, do you like our . . . our club?" he asked.

The Club! That would be a good name for the class. "I like," she said shyly. "And you?"

"I think it could be very good. Me, I could use help. People always say to me 'what, what, what did you say?'"

María Luisa could not quite understand Peter, but she guessed what he was saying and let it go at that. There was a way in which his voice seemed to go up and down that made it different and appealing.

"Do you live here?" he asked.

She nodded and he said, "Good! We can walk together then. How was your paper on WHO I AM?"

"I wrote only a little. I think it could be a big book, that subject, WHO I AM."

"That's my trouble. I could write an' write an' there still would be so much to say. Do you think I talk too much?"

"No, I like," María Luisa answered. Yes, she liked to hear him talk and she liked him to walk beside her. It made her wonder how different they must look. Now she could see that he was quite tall. His straight blond hair kept getting in his eyes and he had to shake his head to get it out of the way; that was charming, she thought. She liked the knit cap he wore and the long scarf wound around his neck. She liked the way his eyes, which were sometimes gray and sometimes blue, seemed to settle on her. She wondered if the world looked different if you looked through gray eyes instead of dark brown ones.

Just then she saw Juan come running up the street to her and she certainly didn't want him to see her talking to a boy, so she said quickly and softly, "Adiós. I have to go now."

"I'll see you tomorrow. Don't forget," he said.

She smiled and then broke away. "Tomorrow" was a beautiful word.

CHAPTER FIFTEEN

"I think you are looking a little happier these days," Uncle Emilio told María Luisa one morning at breakfast. It was the only meal he could share with his family except for his day off. María Luisa had told him about the experimental class, but she was careful not to mention Peter Jensen's name.

"Is all Chicanos in the class?" Uncle Emilio wanted to know.

"No, there's a Greek boy, and some Japanese girls and a Chinese boy and one Danish boy," she passed over that last bit of information rapidly. "The rest are Chicano. The teacher speaks Spanish, too."

"She's Mexican?"

"No, I don't think so. She speaks good Spanish but you can tell she's a foreigner at it. She has little troubles sometimes and we have to tell her the right words, but I guess that's how I am in English. I can speak a little but it's hard to get the words right."

"Don't worry, little one. You're getting prettier all the time. You are prettiest when you're not so sad." He pinched her cheek affectionately. It was good to know that he liked her. Even if he didn't understand how she felt about school, still he gave her the feeling that he was strong and would take care of her.

Classes in school were still impossible, except for Miss Montez's science class, but at the end of each day, like dessert after a meal, was The Club. It made the rest of school worthwhile, just to be part of that class.

When she woke up a few mornings later, she felt odd. She did not feel ill, but rather different. Then she noticed the bloodstains on her nightgown. So it had happened at last. This was her period.

Before she left San Luis, her mother had told her it would be happening, so that she wouldn't become frightened as other girls did when they did not understand what was happening. It happened to all girls. It meant that now María Luisa would become a woman and someday she could have babies.

She sat up in the early dawn and thought about it. So she was growing up! This proved it. Yet she still felt like a child. How odd it was not to be a child any more, yet not to be grown-up either. She looked at Elena lying in her bed, gently curved in sleep. She was fifteen, not at all a child, yet so much more grown-up than María Luisa.

"I'll never be grown-up like Elena," she thought, and wondered what she would be like when she became older.

When she heard Aunt Rosa stirring in the kitchen as she made cereal for Rosita, María Luisa got out of bed and tiptoed to the kitchen over the cold floor. Mama had told her to tell Aunt Rosa when it happened. She whispered the news in Aunt Rosa's ear, blushing a little as she did so, and Aunt Rosa kissed her.

"You're a young lady now! You're growing up!"

Then she showed María Luisa how to take care of herself, how to wash out the bloodstains, and how to mark the date on the kitchen calendar each month with the tiniest, hardly visible initials, so that she would know when to expect it again.

María Luisa was relieved that Aunt Rosa was discreet and did not talk about it to anyone. Still, she wondered if Uncle Emilio knew, for at breakfast he seemed to look at her more than usual and once or twice nodded his head as though he were approving of her. But he did not say a word, and it was unlikely she would ever know.

CHAPTER SIXTEEN

The class was beginning to change. For one thing everyone began to speak to one another while waiting for Miss Stein instead of sitting quietly alone. The discussions that Miss Stein tried to stimulate were still quiet and there were still a few students who hadn't said anything, but now instead of being a group of dull klunkheads, certain students were beginning to speak out and emerge as individuals.

It was not all a matter of talking or writing either. For example, Riko had what Miss Summer would have called busy fingers. During discussions while she listened, her fingers seemed to fold and tear and refold the yellow lined paper for writing, a math worksheet, or language paper. When she was through, she would unfold the paper and there would be an intricately cut bird or flower, a turtle or a fish.

"Show it to everyone, Riko. It's lovely! What clever fingers you have!" Miss Stein had spoken in such spontaneous admiration, that everyone had turned to look and Riko had burst into a cascade of giggles.

"Won't you teach us all how to do it?" Miss Stein asked, and with Riko's patient directions, tried to make it herself. But for all Riko's good will, half the members of the class came out with bits of torn paper.

Another individual was Steve Muñoz, the small boy who always talked about his brother and seldom about himself. It was always, "my brother, Carlos, who was the best basketball player," or "my brother, Carlos, who's a Marine in Vietnam," or "my brother he always say this,"; he implied that whatever his brother did or thought was right. Not everyone agreed, and one afternoon there was a discussion that almost became a fight.

"My brother in Vietnam, he says . . ."

Whether Steve's brother's heroic feats had become too much for everyone or whether it was that explosive word, Vietnam, there were suddenly no more klunkheads. Everyone had something to say.

"He shoulda stayed home. We aw'reddy lost the war, oney the gov'ment don't wanna say it."

"We gonna win. Jus' a little more time. My brother says . . ."

Steve was shouted down. Tears rose in his eyes as he defended his brother's honor.

"How long ya think this war will go on? Till we're all old and dyin'."

"They ain't fightin' any more. They all on hard stuff, man."

"They want to sen' all the Chicanos over there, get rid of 'em. Can't you see, man?"

Riko's high voice was tiny but insistent. Finally everyone listened. "Amel—American can't win war in Asia, not wit' China. Never. Cost too much anyway."

The words came out in tiny jerks, but it was the longest sentence she had spoken. María Luisa did not know as much as the others seemed to, but she had an opinion, too.

"I don' like any war. I am for peace!"

Steve was still fighting the battle single-handedly. Bravely he threw off his attackers, but the fight had become a loud verbal battle in Spanish. Miss Stein reminded them softly that here they were supposed to try to talk English. It was then that Alex spoke out. The heated argument had given him the courage he needed. Nevertheless, he spoke in English.

"Miss Stein, I speak Spanish. My family speak Spanish. I am not ashamed for my language. I want to be wit' my family and wit' my people and fight in *Spanish* if I want. So I don't know why I am here."

Before Miss Stein could answer, Peter spoke up. "Sure, you speak Spanish. Is very good. Nobody says anything against your language. But if you want to tell me how you feel about the war or anyt'ing, I can't understand Spanish. You don't understand Danish. So we both learn the English and we can talk together."

"Miss Stein, I can't understand that guy. Why don' he speak English?"

"Why *doesn't* he," Miss Stein corrected him. "Peter *does* speak English and he speaks well, but he has trouble because he hasn't been around enough people who do speak English. Maybe he has a hard time understanding you, too. Peter, will you please repeat what you said very carefully, because you put it very well."

"I have bad accent, I know that for sure," he said, and then he repeated in essence what he had said before and when he mispronounced his words too badly, Miss Stein corrected him.

Riko, who could be very shy, surprised everybody by standing up and giving a short sparkling speech in Japanese, ending it in a delicious spurt of giggles. Her eyes were bright as she knew what she was doing. She was illustrating Peter's argument.

It gave María Luisa the courage to say something.

"See, if we have to learn Danish to talk to Peter, and Japanese for Riko, and Greek for Tassos and Chinese for Charlie Sun, *Dios mío,* the rest of our life we'd be doing this thing. Easier to learn English. Anyway, we don't have to forget our Spanish, just because we speak English."

That was a long speech for María Luisa and her heart beat wildly. Miss Stein made a little applause sign to her, but could hardly talk because now everyone was sounding off. Finally she asked if she could talk. Imagine a teacher asking permission to say something!

"I'm glad that you brought up the whole matter, Alex, and I'm pleased that all of you seem to care. Understand this, please. Your native language, whatever it is, is a precious thing; that's why they call it your mother tongue, because it is close to you like your mother. It would be wrong for you to forget it and you mustn't think for an instant that that is what we are doing. In fact you should all be reading books in your language, Spanish, Greek, Danish, whatever. Now then, I'd like to hear from Tassos. We don't hear the Greek language very often. Do you think you could recite a Greek poem or tell a story, anything at all in Greek?"

Tassos, who had been very quiet through this, shuffled

101

to his feet and his voice became strong as he recited in Greek. María Luisa felt as though she were seeing him for the first time, even though she did not comprehend a word of his talk.

In turn Ruth Kimura quoted a child's poem in Japanese. Charlie Sun sang a Chinese song. Then Peter, who obviously loved to be in the center of the stage, stood up, held everyone's attention and then spoke earnestly and intensely in his native tongue while everyone sat spellbound. María Luisa thought he must be quoting a love poem. Suddenly he could keep his face straight no longer and burst into laughter at the class.

"You are all so sad and serious. That was an advertisement for *beer!*"

"No fair!" Gloria called out.

"Alex, let's hear this Spanish language you love so much," Miss Stein said.

He stood proudly and waited until the room was absolutely silent.

"*Amigos,* my friends," he said, "Spanish is our language. It is ancient. It is beautiful. It belongs to us and we will never forget it."

"You'll be a politician yet! That was first rate," Miss Stein said. "Did you notice how each language had its own rhythm? Each one had its own particular way of sounding. I thought they were all beautiful. It was like listening to different musical instruments."

Then it was time to write. Usually Miss Stein let the students choose any subject at all, but on that day, she asked them to write about why they thought it was important to learn English.

102

María Luisa found it easy. How could a person hope to get a job in a country where he did not know the language, or to read its newspapers or to talk with anyone who did not speak Spanish? To herself she thought, "It would mean I couldn't talk with Peter." But she knew better than to put that in writing.

That afternoon after walking home with Peter, as she climbed the stairs, she could hear Aunt Rosa scolding Roberto because he had brought home another stray cat. Aunt Rosa was not really angry, but her voice was vibrant with feeling.

"How many cats do you bring home, Roberto? It's not enough that you bring home twenty cats a week; but you find only those cats that have a city of fleas on their backs and cats who don't know how to behave in a house. And who has to clean up after them? Roberto? That's a joke. It's always the *mamá* who has to clean up, wipe up the floor, wipe up the milk, wipe up in the corners everywhere. No, Roberto, I'm through. No more cats. You understand? Well, this one does look hungry. Give it some milk and then take it out. OUT OF THE HOUSE!"

It was a familiar argument and María Luisa had heard it before. Roberto was forever bringing home cats who were invariably full of fleas. Aunt Rosa always scolded him, but she always felt sorry for the cats and fed them anyway.

This time María Luisa did not listen to the meaning of Aunt Rosa's words but to the sound of the Spanish. It had a flowing quality, sometimes short and staccato and sometimes fast, like music; it all emerged easily, like water in a

103

brook tumbling down a mountainside. María Luisa stood in the doorway and listened.

"*Dios mío*," she thought, "all my life I hear Spanish, but now I listen to it for the first time. Yes, it *is* beautiful. And to think it took an English class and Miss Stein who isn't even Spanish, to make me see it!"

CHAPTER SEVENTEEN

Everything was getting better. True, it was not as fast as María Luisa would have liked, but it was obvious enough so that the Nuñez family could see the difference. On one of Uncle Emilio's nights off when the whole family sat around the dining-room table, Aunt Rosa teased María Luisa gently.

"You have secret smiles, María Luisa. There must be a young man somewhere to make you smile like that. . . ."

"Oh, Aunt *Rosa*, what a thing to say!" she became red with confusion.

Elena looked amused, the little boys grinned, and Mike said with mock seriousness, "She has to ask me first if she can have a boy friend. I'm her big brother now."

Uncle Emilio, pleased that María Luisa no longer looked as miserable as she did before, sang fragments of a Mexican love song to her, his eyes twinkling. It was all right to joke with the Santos children because they had almost become part of the family, making jokes and taking part in the conversation almost as much as their cousins. San Luis was all but forgotten.

María Luisa blushed, but no matter how they tried, nobody could get a word out of her. To herself she thought, How lucky I am! First there was nothing but blackness and now there are two bright stars. Miss Stein . . . Peter. How different they are from each other! How lucky I am to know them!

María Luisa had a long way to go to solve all her problems. The next day classes seemed more difficult than ever, and her English teacher scolded her until only the most stubborn determination kept her from bursting into tears. She was learning, but not fast enough.

There was another problem, too. Money. Christmas was coming and she wanted to send a present to her mother. Besides she needed money for stockings and underwear. Aunt Rosa, guessing her predicament, said she could help her. Could she sew? Oh, yes indeed, Sister Celeste had seen to that part of her education. All right, Aunt Rosa had more than enough work to keep her busy; she would pay María Luisa to hem dresses. María Luisa was too young to go out to work, but there was no reason why she couldn't do some at home.

"Aunt Rosa, I don't feel too well. I think maybe I am getting a cold," she said the next morning, trying to convince herself that it wasn't just facing another day of classwork that was too much. "Do you think I could stay home and do some of that hemming?"

"Of course! Stay home! One day won't matter and we'll have a good time together," Aunt Rosa said. She made it so easy.

"I'd miss The Club and Miss Stein," María Luisa considered with some regret. But to spend a day without straining to understand English hour after hour was too much of a temptation. She'd make money too, a day's wages. She could even watch TV if she liked. She put on an old bathrobe of Elena's and sat down at the table while Rosita crawled on her lap and wanted to play patty-cake. Yes, this was so much better than school. She wished she'd thought of it before.

Grandmother brought her a cup of warm milk and a *pan dulce*. While Aunt Rosa spread the dresses to be sewn on the table, she began to tell stories, one after the other, about what it was like when she and María Luisa's mother were girls. María Luisa thought that someday it would be good to write these down. She couldn't do it right now because she was eager to do as much hemming as she could so she could make lots of money. The dresses were unbelievably wide. What kind of ladies were so fat that they could wear such dresses? Two, maybe three, María Luisas could fit into one of those dresses. The morning slipped by quickly when Aunt Rosa told stories, but slowed down to a crawl when she had to go to the store for a minute or take care of Rosita. After lunch, Aunt Rosa had to go to the dentist and *Abuelita* and Rosita took naps, so María Luisa sat alone.

The TV would keep her company and what's more, she could choose any channel she wanted. But there was only a silly contest on one channel and a foolish game on another. She turned off the set. How could adults be so stupid? She sighed and went back to her hemming. When she finished one dress, there was another waiting. "This is so boring!" she cried in exasperation as she picked up another one of the hateful dresses. The work Aunt Rosa did required skill and Aunt Rosa had that . . . everyone said she sewed like an angel . . . but this endless hemming gave no thanks at all.

She wondered if Peter missed her. He was different from everyone else; he looked different, with his lanky build, the straight blond hair and even with his clothes —the blue turtleneck sweater he wore and the peculiar sailor's cap which sat back jauntily on his head. It seemed to fit him; it was a kind of signature that belonged to him. It was the fashion to wear things that were odd, yet everyone made fun of Peter. María Luisa remembered two separate occasions when someone had made cutting remarks; he had laughed right back at them. It took the sting out of the insult, but María Luisa could see that for all the show he put on of not caring, he was really hurt. She almost told him not to worry about it, but then he would have known that she understood, so she said nothing. If only she could laugh and stand up straight as though nothing could hurt her when Elena or others made fun of her, what a help that would be, but, no, she always seemed to shrink inside herself. Miss Stein once said that Peter had style, whatever that was.

As she stopped to change the thread, she thought, "I wonder what they are doing in class now. I wonder what they are saying in The Club. I wonder if anyone misses me. . . ."

With each stitch, she detested hemming a little more. "It would be so much more fun to be writing stories," she thought. The stories Aunt Rosa had told her that morning were enchanting. If they were not written down, they might disappear and that would be a pity.

"*Caray*, I'd rather write than sew, that's for certain," she thought. By two o'clock María Luisa stopped envying Aunt Rosa her easy life and by two thirty she no longer cared if she did have to listen to English all day long from one cross teacher after another. Anything, even that, would be better than spending a lifetime hemming dresses for fat ladies.

The little boys were coming home from school. She could hear them scuffling up the stairs. She gave them milk and crackers, as Aunt Rosa had asked her to do, and then, as they went out to play she reminded Juan, "Remember, we have our reading lesson at four thirty. Don't forget."

She hugged him very hard, for she could still feel the unhappiness in him every day when he came home from school. An hour or so playing out of doors with the boys and then the lesson with her could bring the smile back to his dark eyes once more. She could have wept, however, for his long miserable hours in school. Aunt Rosa had gone to the principal and asked if Juan could be put in José's class, because José's teacher could speak Spanish and she could understand how hard it was for little children who came from a home where only Spanish was spoken. José was happy, but the principal had refused to put Juan in his class. "If we did it for you, we'd have to do it for everyone," she had replied tartly to Aunt Rosa.

María Luisa listened to the boys. Juan was quieter than

his cousins and often seemed worried, but as José made a joke and the boys began to laugh, she was relieved. They were cute little boys, playful as little puppies. If only it weren't for Juan's mean teacher . . .

With a sigh she went back to her hemming.

"*Dios mío,* I'll be back in school tomorrow. That's for *sure!*" she promised.

CHAPTER EIGHTEEN

Each day Miss Stein thought of something different to do or something new to talk about. With each new idea, someone who had previously sat silently seemed to come to life.

One afternoon she began the session by telling The Club about an incident she had seen that morning. "I was at another school and I happened to see a student who was sent to the office because he was late. Actually he had a good excuse, but when he stood before the secretary he stammered and became so shy that he couldn't say a word. He received a pretty bad scolding and a few black marks when he really didn't deserve it. Perhaps some of you have had difficulties like that?"

Paul Ramos raised his hand, blushing as he did so. Gloria Sanchez looked up, but hardly found the courage to admit that she suffered from this kind of shyness, too.

"Sometimes I think it happens to all of us," Miss Stein said. "Perhaps if we act out what we should have done, it will help us. Let's act out this little scene I told you about. Anyone want to be secretary?"

Riko raised her hand. Paul was too shy to act out the part of the student but Ralph was willing.

They arranged a desk in front of the room and Riko sat at it, imitating the prissy manner of the school secretary so unmistakably that everyone giggled a little. However, she caught a syrupy kindness in the secretary's manner.

"Well, Ralph, you are rate . . . I mean, late," she cooed. Riko still had trouble with her r's and her l's, but she was beginning to tell the difference.

Ralph surprised everyone, for he wasn't as shy as he seemed. He pretended to fumble around and then spoke out.

"It's like this, miss, my gran'father hit my gran'mother wit' a ax and they took my gran'mother to the hospital because there was blood all over an' she was all messed up, and then the fuzz come for my gran'father. . . ."

María Luisa sat back shocked, not only at the story Ralph was spinning, but because he seemed to be enjoying it so. Could it be true or was he putting on a good show? He was just serious enough to suggest that such a thing might have happened at some other time. The look on Miss Stein's face which had been amused at Riko's performance had now become concerned. When the little performance was over, however, she went on with the class.

"All right, Paul, you try it this time, would you? The excuse doesn't have to be as colorful as Ralph's."

Paul shuffled to his feet slowly, but acted out the little drama without too much difficulty and only a minor bit of stammering. His excuse was simple and probable; his mother was ill and he had had to dress his little sister and take her to kindergarten. Even in front of a sympathetic Riko, he had difficulty relating the excuse, but he saw it through.

"There, it wasn't so hard, was it?"

"Not here."

"If that or any other occasion like it comes up, you'll be surprised at how well you can manage it."

Miss Stein thought it might be good to act out any other situations they could think of. For a while there was silence and then María Luisa spoke up in a soft uncertain voice.

"My little brother, Juan, he has a mean teacher. Is terrible; everyday he come home sad. My aunt went to talk with the principal to change him to the other first-grade class where is good teacher, but the principal say no. So this is what I think; if my uncle, who is big man, will go to the principal with my aunt, then maybe she will put Juan in the class with the nice teacher."

"That sounds possible, especially if your uncle explains how unhappy Juan is. What's the problem, María Luisa?"

"I'm afraid to ask my uncle. I almos' did once, but you know, I couldn't do it when the time came."

"All right, let's act it out."

This time Alex Alvarez, who knew Uncle Emilio, offered to play his role. He thrust his flat tummy forward, hummed a little song under his breath the way Uncle Emilio did, and pretended to be brushing an imaginary speck of dust off his embroidered jacket.

"Please, Uncle Emilio, could I ask you something?"

"*Sí, mi hijita,* what is it?"

"It's about Juan. He is sad. He don't like his teacher."

"So what little boy likes his teacher or school anyway?"

Alex pretended to wax his mustache. Imitating Uncle Emilio was a great temptation and Alex overacted, but he did it so well that even María Luisa found herself giggling.

"It's just that if *you* went to see the principal, I think she would listen to you and put Juan in José's class."

"If you can do that, you're probably not as scared as you think," Miss Stein said. "I hope you'll try it at home and let us know how it works out."

Simple as it was, the little rehearsal gave María Luisa the courage she had lacked before. The next morning after breakfast, she approached Uncle Emilio as he was fussing with his tie, patting it so it was exactly as he wanted it. He was humming just as Alex had foreseen, but he wasn't the comic figure Alex had made of him. He was a kind man and more concerned than even María Luisa had expected.

"You wanna talk with me? Come, sit down. What you wanna talk about?"

María Luisa told him how unhappy Juan was at school and how Aunt Rosa had gone to see the principal and how she hardly listened to her.

"*Sí,* I know all this. So it's settled. What do you want me to do?"

María Luisa looked down, not wanting to be insistent. Her voice quavered it had become so weak, but she turned to Uncle Emilio even so.

"Juan is so unhappy, I worry for him. He tried to run away once, remember, and he could try again. Sometimes I think so. So it's a special case and not like the principal would have to do it for everybody. If you went to school and told this to the principal, then maybe she would put Juan in José's class."

"Ah, José's class! It's almost too good. He don't care if he learns to read or write. I wish you would give him lessons like you give Juan. After all, it's important for a boy to read and write well."

María Luisa had the words on the tip of her tongue, "And why isn't it important for a girl, too?" but this was not the time to bring that up. Besides, she had another idea.

"I'll be glad to teach José. I think it would be good company for Juan, too."

Uncle Emilio grinned, showing a row of even white teeth.

"You're a good girl, María Luisa," he said and was about to get up to leave when María Luisa put her hand on his sleeve.

"Please, Uncle Emilio, I will teach him if you will go to the school and talk to the principal about Juan."

"Me go to school? That's not for the man to do; it's for the woman. Aunt Rosa's already done this."

"I know, but if you went, you are big and strong and I think you could make the principal understand how it is with Juan."

"Me, go by myself to the principal?"

María Luisa suppressed a smile. Big Uncle Emilio frightened of a school principal!

"Aunt Rosa would go with you, I think. The two of you could explain."

"And this is the price for José's lessons? You drive a hard bargain."

"You can do it. You can try. Would you, please?"

He chuckled, patted her on the head, and then groaned. "*Mañana,*" he said. And she went off to school wondering if he would or not.

The next day when she came home from school, Juan came running to meet her. José followed close behind. "María Luisa, they did it. They changed my teacher. Now I'm in José's class!" His eyes shone with relief.

Aunt Rosa confided in María Luisa. "It wasn't easy getting your uncle to school. It was like driving a donkey where he doesn't want to go. But when the principal pulled up her nose and said no, he got mad, real mad. I never saw him like that before. But the principal listened. So now is no trouble. He's in José's class."

María Luisa could not stop smiling. Some things worked out all right after all. She decided she'd write a letter to her mother that night, after the class with Juan and José. Her mother would like that bit of news.

CHAPTER NINETEEN

Aunt Rosa and Uncle Emilio were more grateful than ever to María Luisa since she began to teach José, but living with Elena was no easier than it had been before. María Luisa knew what to expect of her cousin. She would tease her and make fun of her in sly ways, until María Luisa came close to tears or in a fit of anger would cry out, "Shut up!" after which she would feel worse than ever. When Elena brought her to that point, then she would become soft and sweet and act as though she were her best friend. At such times she really seemed to like María Luisa. Then there were other times, like that night when she sat at the trunk, biting her pencil as she tried to work out a math problem. Elena kept turning up her transistor radio and interrupting María Luisa, until she wanted to scream.

"Writing something for your wonderful Miss Stein and the wonderful *Club*? Boy that name gets me, *The Club*. Why don't they call it what it is, remedial reading or dumbbell English? Don't think I don't know what goes on down there."

What did Elena know? What did she mean? Nothing unusual had happened there. Then María Luisa understood. Elena was teasing, hoping to pull a confidence out of her.

As for the name, The Club, Peter had used it one day in a joking manner, but like many jokes it was taken seriously. After all, nobody came up with a better name and *Language Communication* which came closest to describing it, was too forbidding. So it became The Club. There was a special feeling about belonging to it, too. Now when María Luisa walked through the halls, there were at least a dozen people who might say "Hi!" or "Hello!" to her, and Alex always gave her a slow wink. It was better than it had been before when nobody even looked at her.

María Luisa herself was changing. Now when Elena talked about her boy friends, boasting how Jim had a sports car or Carlos's father was rich, María Luisa listened politely but was no longer jealous. Elena, sensing this, screamed at her.

"You're getting too good for the rest of us, aren't you? I know about your marvelous club, and your marvelous Miss Stein, and I know about Peter, too."

María Luisa turned red and her heart beat in double time. "What do you know about him? What is there to know about him?"

Elena snickered. "Never mind," and she began to file her nails. "Maybe you're just getting too good for this family. What's the matter with a Chicano boy friend? Won't any of them look at you?"

"I don't have any boy friends at all," María Luisa said and then she buried her face in her hands as though that was the end of the conversation. It was true that she liked

Peter and that he walked home from school with her, but then it was on the way to his house. She could say it didn't mean anything. He wasn't a boy friend in the sense that Elena suggested. But there was no use explaining; Elena would never understand.

"You're not such a simple little country cousin any more. I think I liked you better before," Elena said spitefully and she slammed the door as she left the room.

As if that were not enough, on another afternoon Mike knocked on her door as she corrected a story she had written. He had been practicing his guitar and María Luisa had been listening to its delicate cadences when he broke off with three intense chords.

"I want to talk with you," he said.

"Please do. I never see you any more. But I hear the guitar. You are getting better all the time."

From the look on his face, she knew he hadn't come to seek compliments but had something to say, something serious. "He's really beautiful, more like Elena than I had thought," María Luisa said to herself as his dark eyes, usually liquid and calm, now seemed to flash.

"Remember once I said I would be your big brother. I wasn't exactly kidding. I hear that you're going around with that Danish kid."

"I don't 'go around with him.' We're in the same class at school and he walks home the way I do. That's all."

"You know enough not be going around with any Anglos. I'll be patient with you because you're still new here. But I'm warning you, forget this kid."

"Why should I? He's a very nice person and he's very decent. *Caray,* you couldn't find a nicer person."

"It doesn't look right. Besides, you're going to get hurt one way or another. This isn't San Luis, you know."

"If only you knew him, you wouldn't say such things. Anyway, it's not as though I had dates with him. I don't *go* anywhere. You know that."

"What's the matter with some other friends, like brown-skinned friends?"

With that, he left and soon María Luisa could hear the haunting guitar melodies once more. Through the window she could see the city lights beginning to turn on below. How could Peter hurt her? The idea was ridiculous.

It was on the very next day on their way home from school, that Peter asked her if she would like to go to the Park and Aquarium with him the following Saturday.

CHAPTER TWENTY

There was always a great deal for Peter and María Luisa to talk about. They might have stood on the corner talking all day. Occasionally María Luisa would say, "I have to go now," but somehow a full half hour might slip by before she actually did run home.

What did they talk about? Miss Stein, The Club, and each other for the most part.

"It's not so hard to understand you any more, Peter. To tell you the truth, at first I didn't know what you were saying."

"I tell you the truth, too, then. Since a long time I couldn't understand you either. Now most of what you say is not too hard to get."

They had Miss Stein to thank for that. In addition to the talking sessions and the writing, she managed to talk privately with all the members of The Club. Peter's most obvious difficulty was his pronunciation; María Luisa's greatest problem after grammar and word order, was getting used to thinking in English. She did not know she had an accent until Peter had to ask her to repeat what she had said. Then Miss Stein helped her to see what she was doing wrong. She learned to say "this" instead of "thees" and to pronounce a final "er" without rolling the "r."

Peter's ideas extended far beyond the limits of The Club and school. On that particular Friday he was telling María Luisa about some new fish that had been sent to the Aquarium in Golden Gate Park.

"Aquarium? What is it, Aquarium? I been to the Park but I never see it," she said.

"You haven't seen it? Oh, you must see it, you must. Let's go tomorrow. My mother can make sandwiches for us. Do you like Danish sandwiches?"

"I never had one."

"You will tomorrow. Will you come?"

Her eyes brimmed with excitement. She hadn't been anywhere since the first weekend she had arrived and once or twice when Elena asked her to go shopping. She was about to say yes, but she remembered Mike's warning. She knew that she should ask Aunt Rosa, but what if she were to say no. She smiled at Peter as she hesitated, trying to think of what to do. Finally she decided that just this once she would go and not tell anyone.

At that moment Juan and José came by pulling a wagon in which a plump and grinning Rosita sat like a little princess. As soon as the boys saw Peter and María Luisa, they lost no time in making fun of them.

"María Luisa's got a boy friend!"

"Kiss and hug! Kiss and hug!"

If looks could kill, the two little boys would have lain on the sidewalk as two corpses, María Luisa was that angry with them. Peter, trying to suppress a smile though his eyes twinkled, made it a little easier for María Luisa.

"What are they saying? I don't understand Spanish."

How innocent he looked, just as though he had not understood every word!

"I will meet you here tomorrow at nine thirty on the corner. OK?" she whispered, hoping the boys hadn't heard.

"Good! That's a date!" he answered.

Then María Luisa went home.

But the boys had overheard and they told Aunt Rosa. "It's none of your business and I don't like tattletales," she scolded them.

Aunt Rosa spoke to María Luisa later that night when they were in the kitchen cleaning up after dinner.

"You think I don't know about it? You have a date and you don't want anyone to know. I know. Once I was a girl myself."

María Luisa turned her head away so Aunt Rosa would not see her blush. On the other hand, she was relieved not to have to lie about it.

"Peter wants to take me to the park so I can see the Aquarium. His mother will make sandwiches. He's so nice, Aunt Rosa. I know he would never hurt me. Never."

"Well, all right, this once. But you must do the right thing. First you bring him here and introduce him. That is the respectful way to act."

"He is an Anglo."

"Yes, yes. You think I haven't seen him talking with you on the corner? It doesn't make that much difference. A good person is a good person. But first he must come here to meet us and then it must be understood you are home by four thirty in the afternoon, no later."

María Luisa could hardly believe it. She had expected more opposition from Aunt Rosa than anyone else, and instead, Aunt Rosa understood.

"Here's a dime, María Luisa. Go to the grocery store and use the phone there. Call Peter and tell him to come here first. That is the right way. You understand?"

"Oh, yes! Aunt Rosa, you are such an angel!" María Luisa threw her arms around her aunt and hugged her. Everything was going to be all right after all.

CHAPTER TWENTY-ONE

"But why do you make such a big thing out of it? We're only going for a walk in the park," María Luisa protested. "It's just a project for science class," she added feebly.

"How the dear old Junior High has changed! When I went there, boys and girls didn't go to the park for science projects! Here, try this on!"

Elena looked through her drawers and pulled out a rosy pink sweater and threw it on María Luisa's bed. Elena might not understand The Club and she might not understand María Luisa, but she knew all about dates. Now that Aunt Rosa approved, she wanted to be responsible for showing off María Luisa at her best. To please her cousin, María Luisa tried on sweaters, dresses, and even Elena's good coat, but in the end she wore her own everyday skirt with the white turtleneck sweater.

Everyone had something to say about the occasion, even *Abuelita* who warned María Luisa that in her day a girl always had a chaperone but nowadays . . . she had broken off in mid-sentence, shaking her head in disapproval.

Peter arrived at nine thirty sharp. The house had been carefully dusted and straightened and the pillows fluffed up. There was a long awkward silence as everyone sat around staring at Peter. Her voice betraying her nervousness, María Luisa introduced him to everyone. He *is* charming, she thought as Peter said a few words to each, shook hands with the three little boys who hardly said a word, having been gravely warned by Aunt Rosa that they were to be on their best behavior *or else.* Rosita flirted with Peter and this gave everyone a chance to smile and relax a little. Even Mike, who had been glowering all morning, shook hands with Peter. Then, an uncomfortable silence.

Aunt Rosa broke it with an awkward attempt at humor.

"It's a beautiful day, but if you don't get started, I think maybe your fish will swim away. Don't forget now. Home by four thirty."

The ordeal was over. Released, the two of them fled down the stairs into the winter sunshine. It was a day like a song and María Luisa wished it would last forever.

CHAPTER TWENTY-TWO

They flew down the street, caught the bus just as it was pulling out, and sat together in back, a little out of breath. Now that they had all day to talk, they could think of nothing to say. They grinned foolishly at each other but did not speak.

As they walked through the park to the Aquarium, María Luisa felt centuries removed from the wide-eyed little girl who had first seen the park only last September. Now as she walked under the tall trees, hurrying a little to keep up with Peter's long stride, she felt content. She needed nothing more to make her happy.

Actually she was not quite sure what an aquarium was. In the science room at school there was a small glass tank with tiny fish which Miss Montez had set up. María Luisa was not prepared for anything as overpowering as the great tank with its dolphins and seals. The pit in which alligators slept or smiled wickedly while people stared down from the iron fence above was a nightmarish scene.

"They make me cold to look at them, those alligators. I

think they would smile while they bit off your leg," María Luisa said.

When they turned around, they saw a tank full of sea-horses.

"Peter, those cute little things! Look at them! They're living."

"Sure, they're alive! What did you think they were, toys?"

"Well, I saw some the kids drew in art class and I thought like they were designs. I never knew they were real things. I wish I could bring some home to the boys."

"They'd lock you up and throw away the key," Peter whispered.

"OK. So I won't take one. Not today," she answered lightly.

He could hardly tear her away from them, but soon they were walking through dark corridors lined on both sides with lighted tanks full of fish. It was another world. "Like walking under the sea," María Luisa whispered to Peter. Where the fish swam so silently, it seemed as though it should be a hushed world. Each group of fish was entirely different from the one they had just seen; it might be the striping or the shape or the total effect, as though each family of fish were a separate creation. Some sped by fast and hard as if they were desperate enough to sail right through the glass while others moved slowly as if in a dream. One tank full of darting lights held thousands of tiny transparent fish. It was all quite miraculous.

When they turned a corner, María Luisa saw the reflection of Peter and herself unexpectedly fused with the blue and green waters of a tank, so that they looked as though they were under the sea. Peter saw the reflection, too, and was as spellbound by their strange appearance as was María Luisa. "I *must* remember this," María Luisa thought. "It's important." And yet she could find no reason for doing so.

Coming out into the sunlight again, they found they were hungry. Sounds of band music broke the mysterious atmosphere of the Aquarium. Sure enough, a band was playing a noon concert in the band shell. Peter led María Luisa to the sunken garden that faced the band, and as they sat down on a bench, he said, "Guess what we're having for lunch! Fish sandwiches!"

"Fish sandwich?" María Luisa asked, very doubtful about the whole thing, particularly after having seen a whole houseful of live swimming fish.

"Don't look so funny, it's all OK," Peter told her as he took the wrapped sandwiches from a blue string bag he carried. "It's smoked fish. Sardines from Norway, and here's an eel sandwich like we have in Denmark sometime, and herring. Help yourself!"

María Luisa bit into the sandwich gingerly, but soon brightened.

"I do like very much. It's so good. I never tasted dark bread like this before."

"My mother is . . . how do you say . . . . a 'nut' on nutrition. Seaweed soup, blackstrap molasses, all that."

María Luisa was afraid that the *pan dulce* Aunt Rosa had given her to take along was probably not nutritious. Still it was pretty with its shell-like form and pink icing. Peter found it delicious.

"We don't have good things like this often because my mother's always worrying about getting fat. Me, I'm like my father. Curious. I have to try everything. My father works on a ship so when he's away, my mother and I go together to a French restaurant maybe or a Chinese. We go all over the city. Although, it's not so good as it sounds, really."

"I don't understand, Peter."

"We go out because we don't have a real family. When my father comes home, he stays for two weeks maybe or a month. Then we stay home and my mother makes Danish food, the way he likes, and it's almost like a family."

María Luisa had never heard Peter talk so confidentially before. She did not quite know what he was trying to say.

"A real home is something like the Nuñez family. The mother, the father, even the grandmother and all the kids. And you stay in one place. With us, we always move from one place to the next. It's my father's job for one thing, but my mother likes to go from one place to another. So many places!" he said sadly, almost to himself.

"But you just said you were curious about everything."

"Yes, I am, but sometimes I wish I weren't always a stranger. Just when I begin to make some friends, my mother wants to go somewhere else."

He broke off with a shrug of his shoulders as though he had been talking nonsense and had perhaps said more than he intended.

"I know what you mean, I think," María Luisa said. "I love my family, of course, they are so good to me. But I'm not the same as them; I'm different. They are happy to stay home or if they go out, they only go to friends who are like themselves; and they always speak Spanish. But everything else, the museum or maybe a concert, they don't care. Even if they have a picnic, like we had once, it's like they draw a circle around themselves."

Peter held her hand and looked into her eyes to show

he was really caring about what she was saying. She felt free to go on and to say things she had never told anyone.

"Sometimes at night I like to sit and look out the window at the city. I think there is so much there, so many people, so many things to do. The world is so big and I don't want to be all the rest of my life in one little place, afraid to move. You know what I mean?"

"Yes, because I feel this, too. I guess that both of us want everything, the cage and the freedom, too."

They looked at each other earnestly. Then they were distracted by a plump little boy who stumbled over Peter's long legs on his way to catch a fat pigeon with a purple breast who had had years of experience in getting away from such little boys!

There was all the time in the world that day. They walked. They laughed. At the lake they rented a rowboat.

"You mean you have never in all your life been in a boat?" Peter asked, hardly able to believe such a thing.

"Where was there to go? There was no water in San Luis. You don't take a boat in an irrigation ditch."

But she remembered a Mexican folk song her mother had taught her once about being on the water, and she sang it to Peter. Peter liked the song and begged her to teach it to him.

They rowed past couples in canoes and families in rowboats. Sometimes they passed a family of ducks gliding close to shore in and out of the green rushes that rose out of the water. María Luisa had never seen so many different kinds of ducks. Then Peter let María Luisa row the boat.

"It looks so easy. Can I do it?" she asked. He agreed

and she could not understand the curious smile on his face, as they changed places and he told her how to hold the oars.

She understood soon enough, however, for they kept going in circles. She looked at him in bewilderment. "Please, Peter, help me. We'll be here all day!"

He helped her row to the shore. The sun was disappearing in the rising fog and María Luisa shivered as the day turned cold.

"I know just the thing. Tea in the Japanese Garden," Peter said.

María Luisa had never heard of it, but she walked along with Peter, happy to go anywhere he wanted to go. The day was too full of surprises. María Luisa in Wonderland! They passed through a tremendous oriental gate and entered the greenest garden María Luisa had ever seen. They strolled along a network of walks bordered with bamboo fences. Here and there were stone lanterns, and everywhere there were birds flying. Occasionally squirrels scrambled up the trunk of a twisted tree.

A footbridge circled high in the air so that when its reflection was seen in the brook below, it formed a perfect circle. Together they climbed over it and laughed when by accident they were included in a movie somebody was taking.

"I think everyone in this park has a camera but us," Peter said.

"I don't need a camera. I remember everything in my head and sometimes in my heart." Then she giggled. "That's sentimental, huh?"

"I don't care," he said.

The teahouse was an open wooden structure perched

on the side of a hill. They sat at a tiny table while a Japanese waitress in a brilliantly colored kimono brought them a pot of tea and a plate of cookies. Peter told her that her fortune was inside the curled up cookies, and she should take the first one.

She opened it and took out the tiny slip of paper.

"This is the year of decision for you," it said. She smiled broadly at this, looked serious for a moment, and then shook her head as though it were all too silly. But she put the slip of paper in her bag.

They sat together for a long time, drinking tea out of tiny cups and watching the fog as it gathered in some places and cleared in others. Never had the world seemed more peaceful to María Luisa. She thought, no matter what else happens to me in my life, I have this day and it's a perfect day. Nobody will ever be able to take it away from me.

It was later than they realized and they rushed through the park, caught the bus and by the time they were in front of the house, María Luisa was only a few minutes late.

"Thank you, Peter, it was the most beautiful, wonderful day I ever had."

"Maybe we can do it again. For me it was beautiful, too."

He held her hand tightly for a moment, and then broke off. She watched him stride off before she went upstairs.

CHAPTER TWENTY-THREE

María Luisa was haunted by that day. Every time she thought of it, the sky seemed to have been a little more blue and the grass and trees more intensely green; she herself was far more beautiful and Peter was taller, although she found him quite perfect as he was and not needing any exaggeration. It had been a poetic day, if a day could be poetic.

In math class she leaned on her elbow and looked out the window. Never mind Mr. Thompson droning away up in front; she wouldn't understand him anyway. Poetic days are what she understood. The phrase stuck. She wrote down on the yellow scratch pad in front of her . . .

> *A day like a poem and you and I*
> *walking under a rain-washed sky . . .*

A good start. She wrote down a few more phrases. Then troubles began. Did a poem have to rhyme? She wasn't sure. How did you know if a poem was good or not?

Sometimes a poem came so easy it seemed to write itself out; other times you had to coax it. Well, she'd ask Miss Stein. She would know.

But the chance didn't come up. Steve Muñoz was absent from The Club that day and Miss Stein was worried. "This is the third day he hasn't shown up. He usually comes. Does anyone know what the trouble is?"

"Yeah," Alex said. "You know his big brother, Carlos, the one he was always talking about? Well, he was wounded. His leg got shot off."

The horror on Miss Stein's face reflected the horror everyone felt. "Oh, no," she moaned softly.

María Luisa and Peter looked at each other and then dropped their eyes. Stories of violence and atrocities were common; the TV showed them all the time. But to have this happen to someone they knew, made it seem real. They did not know Carlos, but they knew how Steve felt about him.

"He says he's gonna drop out of school. He ain't comin' back."

"Isn't," Miss Stein corrected Alex absently. She looked upset.

"Isn't. He *isn't* comin' back."

"What's Steve's address, Alex?" she asked and she wrote it down as well as Alex's directions for getting there. It was time to begin the meeting. Somehow nobody felt very much like talking, so Miss Stein suggested they spend the whole time writing.

Immediately after, when they had given Miss Stein their papers, Peter said to María Luisa, "Let's go see Steve. He must feel awful."

Alex overheard them. "Go if you want to, but it don't

132

do no good. He just sits there. He's takin' it real hard."

"We only want to tell him we're sorry," Peter said.

"And say hello and tell him we miss him," María Luisa added.

The two of them followed Alex's directions, down Mission Street, past a few dark alleys that seemed to form a small community of their own, and finally they came to a narrow unpainted house that seemed barely able to stand under its own weight. The upstairs windows were broken and the glass that was left caught the light of the setting sun in its jagged edges. María Luisa and Peter walked through a long dark hallway that smelled of cabbage and old rotting things. Peter knocked on the door at the end of the passage. No answer. He knocked again. Finally María Luisa called out.

"Steve? This is María Luisa and Peter. Can we come in?"

At last the door opened and Steve stood there, short and dark. His face looked stony like the masks carved on ancient Mexican buildings. He motioned for them to come inside and offered them a seat on the sofa, a broken piece of bedding from which a twisted spring and shred of dirty cotton batting protruded.

María Luisa sat gingerly on a wobbly chair while the two boys sat on the sofa. She had never seen any room anywhere that was more depressing. The only light came from a small window at the far end of the room. The floor was patched and seemed damp; here and there a pattern of old worn linoleum emerged. There was no furniture excepting for a few shabby chairs like the one she sat on and a scarred table on which lay an open knife and a comic book. María Luisa stiffened a little with terror because she thought there might be rats. Then she felt ashamed for thinking of her own fears when there sat Steve, his whole attitude one of hopelessness.

Peter spoke. "We just heard about your brother. We came to tell you we are sorry. It's a terrible thing."

Steve nodded. No answer.

"Where is Carlos now, Steve? Is he still there? Have they sent him home?"

"What's it to you?" Steve's voice was belligerent.

"But we do care," María Luisa said and then she began to talk with him in Spanish. "It's a rotten thing to have happened and, well, we know how much your brother means to you."

"All right, so you know," he said gruffly.

"Have you written to him?"

"How should I write? What should I say?"

"It would make him feel better just to hear from you. No matter what you said, he'd know that you care. He needs to know that someone loves him."

"So what do I say? That he can't run any more but you can get by all right with a wooden leg? That he can't play basketball any more but that he can watch others play? You don't know Carlos. Sports are his whole life. Sports and just being a man, I guess."

"Maybe he can't take part in sports any more," said María Luisa, "but there are other things. He can find something else. Think of how he must lie there in the hospital and all the bitter thoughts he must have. Like maybe he feels all alone in the world and nobody cares about him any more."

The door opened and a short heavy woman, her face thick with makeup, came in. Unsmiling she looked at

Peter and then shot a glance to María Luisa, a glance of undisguised suspicion. María Luisa felt a cold chill down her spine. Then without a word the woman disappeared into the dark kitchen, shutting the door behind her.

"Is that your mother?" Peter asked, and Steve nodded. It was easy to see why all Steve's love seemed to center on his brother.

The three of them sat silently in the darkness of the late afternoon. Peter reached over at one point and closed the knife while Steve watched but did not say a word.

There was a knock on the door but before Steve got up to answer it, Alex walked in with Ralph and Jésus. In embarrassed voices they expressed their regrets to Steve, who seemed overcome by so much company. No sooner had the boys sat down when they thought there was a timid knock on the door. Was someone there or not? They listened and the little knock came again. Steve opened the door and there was Riko; Ruth stood a little behind her holding a small bunch of marguerites.

"It's for you, Steve. We are sorry about your brother, and . . ."

The tears rose in Riko's eyes and spilled down her cheeks while Ruth, looking almost as touched, gave Steve the flowers. He was confused, embarrassed by the flowers and touched by the girls' sympathy. "That's OK, Riko. Hey, thanks. Ruth . . ." he hardly knew what to say. He ended by remembering to invite them in. He ran into the kitchen and came back with a chair for them. Then he looked around at all his visitors.

"Hey, did all you guys at The Club plan this?"

"So help me, we didn't."

"Nobody planned anything."

Everyone began to talk, but it wasn't the way it was at The Club. Their voices were subdued and they spoke less freely. There was another knock on the door.

"A real surprise party," Steve said, hardly knowing whether to be bitter or pleased. He wasn't sure he wanted all the sympathy he was getting.

Alex went to the door and this time it was Miss Stein who came in, a box in her hand. She took Steve's hand in her own for a moment.

"Hello, Steve. We've missed you."

At first she wasn't aware of everyone in the room, for it was getting quite dark. Then she recognized Riko and Ruth.

"My goodness, it seems as though we're all here."

The girls made room for her on the sofa and she sat down. Now there was another silence, as they waited for Miss Stein to talk.

"This is some airmail stationery, Steve. I know you'll want to write to your brother right away. When do you think you'll see him again?"

"We aren't sure. He's in a hospital there now, and then he'll have to go to another hospital. We don't even know where it will be." Steve took the box of paper Miss Stein held out and thanked her. He had a hard time talking. As if to help the situation everyone else began to talk even though it was not easy to think of what to say. María Luisa heard Miss Stein talking to Steve.

"Things will work out, better than you think, perhaps. You'll have to be the big brother for a while, if you really want to help him," she said.

Steve seemed thoughtful. María Luisa sensed that perhaps he wanted to be alone with Miss Stein.

"Hey," she said, "it's late. I gotta go. *Caray,* what will my aunt say?"

"Steve," she said as she held out her hand to him. The others shook hands or nodded and murmured, "I'll see you at school," and within ten minutes Steve was left alone with Miss Stein.

On the way home María Luisa said, "Did you notice, nobody said a word about Steve dropping out, just like nobody knew about it? I'll bet anything he comes back to school tomorrow."

"I think so, too. Miss Stein will know just what to say. It might even be a relief to get out of that awful place and go back to school."

"It's a terrible place . . ." María Luisa, unable to think of words to express the misery she had felt there, merely shook her head and Peter understood. "But I think he was pleased that we came. Everyone seemed to care so much, did you notice?"

"Sure. I guess there is really something about having friends. Even people you didn't know were friends. Maybe it really means something."

"Could be," María Luisa said, "but it's late and I'll get too many questions if I don't get home. So, *hasta luego,* Peter!"

And with that she ran up the stairs.

CHAPTER TWENTY-FOUR

February and March had almost flown by and everything was going well. Juan's new teacher made all the difference in the world; now he loved to go to school. María Luisa's mother was getting better every day. School was still difficult, but it did not bother her as much as it had because at the end of classes there was always The Club waiting. Miss Stein had encouraged María Luisa to write and she found herself spending almost all her free time writing. One story seemed to lead to another; one poem invariably gave her an idea for another. She could have stayed up night after night writing, but Aunt Rosa would scold her gently and make her turn out the light and go to sleep. Even so, everything seemed to be going well.

So it was a shock to everyone when another letter from school warned Aunt Rosa that María Luisa was in danger of failing. At The Club that day María Luisa sat staring straight ahead and though she picked up her pen, for the first time since being there, she couldn't write a word.

"What's wrong?" Miss Stein asked.

In a voice close to tears, María Luisa told her.

"But it doesn't make sense at all, María, because you are doing so well here. There must be a reason. You do care, don't you?"

"Oh, yes!" In discussion one day everybody had agreed that the marking system wasn't at all reliable, but Miss Summer had told María Luisa she should try to get good grades so she could go to college.

"Is it the language that bothers you?" Miss Stein asked.

María Luisa shook her head no. She still became lost on occasion, but for the most part she could understand what her teachers said. Maybe she was still something of a "klunkhead." Even when she thought she knew the answer, she was afraid to say anything. If a teacher asked her a question directly, her mind would go blank, the blood would rush to her head, and she would say in a voice that could scarcely be heard that she didn't know, although she might have known perfectly the whole time. All this she tried to explain to Miss Stein. Miss Stein listened and then looked straight into María Luisa's eyes, as though she could look right through her.

"Could it be, María Luisa, that you are a dreamer?"

"Me, a dreamer? I hope not."

The dreamers were easy to spot. They rested their heads on their hands or even on their desks. Their mouths dropped open and their eyes seemed glazed; it was not hard to guess that they were a million miles away. Sometimes they fell asleep. How silly they looked! No, she certainly wasn't a dreamer. Miss Stein wasn't quite so sure.

"Here's something you might do. Next week, every now and then stop and ask yourself if you are really pay-ing attention or if you are a hundred miles away, and see what comes up. All right?"

"Oh, Miss Stein, I'm not a daydreamer," she said, but she agreed to test herself during the week.

Miss Montez announced they were going to make a study of the sun.

"What sun, Teach'?"

"Hey, Miss Montez, we never heard of no sun."

Smiling sympathetically, she held up her hand for silence. Outside the fog had been blotting out the world for over a week. Practically all of María Luisa's teachers had read and recited the same Carl Sandburg poem about the fog that came in "on little cat feet."

Caray, it was a fine poem but had nobody else ever written a poem about a fog? Anyway, this particular fog had never heard of the poem, María Luisa decided. It settled down on its silent haunches and made up its mind to stay forever.

The sun! All Miss Montez had to do was mention the word and a rare remaining lump of homesickness rose in María Luisa's throat. While Miss Montez started by questioning the class about how big the sun was, how far away, where it was located in the universe, all the while drawing diagrams and writing down figures, María Luisa was thinking of the sun. San Luis and sunshine. It seemed farther away than ever. In Arizona the sun had shone everywhere, pouring down generous showers of golden light and warmth on the cornfields and the red peppers, on the little houses and the roads, on the school and on the playground where the children ran and shouted as they played tag and I Spy. As summer came on, the children grew a golden brown and their sharp clear shadows grew black in the heat of the day. When the heat became too oppressive and the sun was too glaring, Miss Summer would let everyone sit outside in the cool shade of the cottonwood trees and then she would read stories to the children and tell them myths. . . .

"Lights out for slides!" Miss Montez's voice had an impatient edge that was not quite normal for her. The class buzzed more loudly than usual. The weather was getting everyone down. Miss Montez indeed seemed annoyed as she explained the charts and diagrams of the sun and stars.

"It's stupid. All those figures. So what do they mean? Nothing to me. Elena is right not to bother with it!" María Luisa thought. She longed to be back in Arizona again, a little child playing jump rope in the sun without all the worries she had found in San Francisco.

"All right, spot quiz everyone. Right now!" Miss Montez snapped as she turned the lights back on. She was in no mood to be trifled with. María Luisa felt nervous as she prepared to take the quiz, and with good reason. Ten questions and she didn't get a single answer right! But she was no Elena, for Elena wouldn't have cared. María Luisa felt as though she wanted to hide in shame.

Caramba! Then she remembered Miss Stein's warning. So she was a daydreamer after all. This proved it.

Miss Montez turned the lights out once more and continued with the slides. María Luisa determined to pay attention, but it was not easy—she didn't really care. Then a slide flashed on the screen, a black circle surrounded by a fiery halo of flames. The sun in eclipse! In a terrible instant she imagined how it happened, the sun blotting out the whole world in darkness. The thought of it made her shudder. How could such things happen?

This time she listened and the diagrams began to make sense. So that's how it happened! The moon passed between the sun and the earth. Astronomers must be very smart, she decided, to figure out just when it would happen. Miss Montez showed more slides. Now she began to get the first idea of what the sun actually was, this enormous burning ball around which the whole earth rolled, day after day, years after year, century after century.

By the time Miss Montez turned the lights on once more, María Luisa found herself almost dizzy thinking about these great movements of the sun and earth that went on all the time without stopping.

On the way home from school, she confessed to Peter her attack of homesickness.

"You really don't want to go back, do you?"

"If I was six years old, yes, but not now, not as I am now. The sun did seem awfully different there. I know, it's one sun, but it keeps changing."

"You're *one* María Luisa and even you keep changing."

She stuck her tongue out at him playfully, and then they decided to have an ice-cream cone. The sun was in the sky over the fog, and with Peter at her side, she was no longer homesick.

CHAPTER TWENTY-FIVE

Finding out that she was a dreamer solved some of María Luisa's problems. All she had to do was stop every time she caught herself and pay attention to the lessons. But it wasn't as simple a matter as it seemed. The lesson on the solar eclipse had been fascinating once she began to listen. In most classes, she preferred her daydreams to the things that were being taught.

Uncle Emilio didn't care if she passed or not; nobody seemed to think it mattered. Elena laughed at her for doing all that writing for Miss Stein and for being so determined to study. She was becoming convinced it would be all right to stop trying. Then a letter would come from Miss Summer or Sister Celeste that would say how fine a student she had always been and they knew she was doing well and would always be proud of her. So then she knew she couldn't really give up.

Math was the biggest monster. Even when she became stern with herself and paid attention, still the results were bad. Mr. Thompson frequently sent five students to the blackboard, each with a problem to solve and explain. The other four would work theirs out and María Luisa would stand in front of hers without the slightest clue as to solving it. If only she could shrink away to nothing and disappear, but no such luck.

"All you have to do is find 'X,' " Mr. Thompson would tell her over and over. But "X" refused to reveal itself. María Luisa would sit down in disgrace and another student would swagger to the board and prove how obvious the answer was.

All right, so I'm the *tonto*, the class dunce, she said to herself. Give up, María Luisa, give up, give up, the little voice tempted her. At the same time she was angry with the elusive "X." "I'll catch you yet, you devil," she promised.

One day a new girl came to class. The poor girl was plain and fat, which meant the boys made fun of her, the girls looked down on her, and the country school from which she came had not prepared her for the unrestrained character of the math class. She was sent to the blackboard with a math problem and there she stood helplessly while the boys whistled and yelled out crude words. María Luisa could feel her misery. She must feel like a helpless rabbit cornered in a field by dogs, she thought. What made it sadder was that she seemed like a good person, a girl who would normally be pink-cheeked, at home making cookies in a clean kitchen or playing jump rope in the street. The one place where she should not be was at that blackboard, a target for a merciless class and Mr. Thompson who was in one of his black moods. Impatient with her, he insisted that she stay at the blackboard until she solved her problem.

María Luisa was full of sympathy. "If only I could help

her. . . ." Her eyes glanced vaguely over the problem on the board and with a suddenness that amazed her, she understood how to solve it.

"I can do it, Mr. Thompson," she yelled, amazed that she could be so loud. Some of the class giggled. This time she did not care.

"All right, María Luisa, you explain it," he said, amused at her excitement in spite of his black mood. As María Luisa walked to the board she heard one boy say, "One dumdum isn't enough. We gotta have two of them together!" She would have said "drop dead" to them, but she was too busy figuring out how the problem could be solved.

First she looked directly at the new girl and smiled at her, hoping she would get the message, "don't be afraid!" Then she took the chalk and explained the problem step by step, amazed that it should be so clear. The boys applauded sarcastically and someone threw a paper airplane at the new girl.

"Don't pay attention to them. They don't matter," María Luisa whispered to the new girl.

And so she found out something else. She was no longer afraid of the boys, or of the math either.

Math was a game. If only she had known before . . . . people could explain it until they were blue in the face or you could study all night long, but understanding was something you had to do by yourself, like riding a two-wheel bike for the first time, or catching on to a joke, or doing one of those wooden Chinese puzzles that seem simple at first, then impossible, and then simple again once you "catch on."

"Learning is a funny thing, don't you think so, Miss Stein? I mean in English it's slow, a little every day. In

145

math, *Dios mío*, it happens like a flash of light. Whoosh! All of a sudden!"

"It seems that way, but you were ready to understand math a long time ago. It didn't work though because you kept fighting against it. Then when you wanted to help that new girl, you didn't have to fight against math any more. So you were able to do it."

"I don't understand."

"Let's put it this way. You've seen a flower bloom. It seems to happen all at once. But you know that first the seed underground had to sprout, and then the stems and leaves had to grow, and not until then was the flower able to blossom. Learning happens like that sometimes. What do you think?"

María Luisa did not really know. It was all very curious.

She expected that from that day on when she had blossomed so brilliantly in math class, the very new problem she faced would be just as easy to understand. Unfortunately, the new ones were every bit as hard as the old ones had been. They still seemed a waste of time.

"That 'X'!" she told Peter. "It's like catching a fish in your hands. One minute it's there, the next minute it's gone. If I ever catch that 'X,' I'll cut his head off him."

"Never mind, someday you'll find your 'X' again," he comforted her. More than once he had helped her with her math homework.

"Someday 'X' and I are going to say *adios* to one another. It will be forever, and there will be no tears, not from me!"

CHAPTER TWENTY-SIX

It was impossible to believe that this had once been a class of klunkheads. Words flew. Ideas bloomed. Vigorous arguments and unexpected alliances came about as everyone wanted to talk at once. Nor was any subject sacred; everyone was developing opinions about everything: race, war, drugs, poverty programs, ecology, food stamps, prisons, space travel, and even on one day the subject of abortion. Ralph said somehow he didn't think it was right to talk about all those things, not with girls around, and everyone jumped on him.

"You can't make believe it ain't there, Ralph. That's being a hypocrite. It's all around us, right here in this school, that and the drugs, the whole thing. It's us we're talkin' about."

Miss Stein did more and more of the listening as time went on. Sometimes she added a quiet word to cool an argument that was getting out of hand or to help when someone could not find the right words.

"She's pleased," María Luisa told Peter and he thought so, too.

"If it weren't for The Club, think how many could have dropped out of school or maybe got hooked on drugs or worse? It's a good thing."

"Peter, you know when Miss Stein talks with us all alone in back of the room, that's supposed to be like a secret, huh?"

"Yeah, why?"

"Nothin' much," she said. Actually she had overhead a conversation between Miss Stein and Gloria. She didn't mean to eavesdrop; she couldn't help hearing.

"You know, you aren't a bad-looking girl, Gloria."

Gloria's eyes fell.

"Do you know you have a sweet face? There are some things that might help. By the way, the sewing teacher says, if you like, she will help you mend your dress so you won't need a safety pin to hold the seam together. Would you like me to arrange a time for you to get together with her?"

Gloria had blushed, but María Luisa didn't hear anything more because she became lost in her own paper. This had happened several weeks ago, but she had noticed that ever since that time, Gloria's dresses were mended and the glaring safety pin had disappeared. María Luisa was aware that something, she could not quite tell what, was happening to Gloria.

The next week Miss Stein thought of something new to do. "You all write ever so much better than when you started. Of course we all have a long way to go, but what would you say for a little change? That is, why don't we all become planners for the next week or two. That is, take something that appeals to you and see what you can do with it. You'll want to say why your plans are a good idea, how it could be done, what's involved, all that. You can plan a city, a gym, a park, a house, anything you like."

"How 'bout growin' chinchillas?" Jesús asked. Everyone groaned. He had been taken with this idea lately and couldn't understand why nobody else was enthusiastic.

"Could I plan something with clothes?" Riko asked. "A city is too big for me."

"Anything at all. You can make drawings to go with it, if you like."

There was a variety of groans, cheers, a rapid scrawling by some and a puzzled pencil-biting session by others. Peter wanted to go to the library and María Luisa went with him.

"Boy, since I am here I never had such ideas, María Luisa! A city. What a city it will be! No cars. Lots of parks and playgrounds. People will learn to walk again. Lots of gyms so everyone keeps in shape."

"I can just see my Uncle Emilio and Aunt Rosa running off to gym!" María Luisa said, but Peter hardly heard her. He checked out an armful of books at the library and on the way home he talked so much, he began to lapse into Danish.

"I've never seen you so happy," María Luisa said.

"I talk too much. I'm sorry. But it's true. I'm happy and I don't even know why. I've thought about it before, but now I am really thinking about it."

After a while, he said, "And I didn't even ask what you are going to do."

"I will show you, but I can't tell you, not yet."

Peter didn't beg her to tell him. In his clear blue eyes the form of the ideal city was beginning to take shape. This was a new Peter.

And in María Luisa's mind she could see a tiny house,

with two canaries in a cage outside the window, and her mother weeding the flower beds and Juan going off to play baseball with his friends and she, María Luisa, sitting at a table inside with a pile of paper in front of her, writing and writing. Were a dream and a plan the same?

On Thursday Miss Stein hurried off twenty minutes early and everyone was surprised to see Gloria get in her little Triumph and sit beside her. What was that all about?

The next day they knew. Gloria came to school, a transformed Gloria. Her hair had been washed, cut, and shaped most likely at a beauty parlor, and she wore a new dress, a simple dark blue dress that was somehow exactly right for her. She sat at her seat and glowed with pleasure as the compliments flew.

"You look wonderful!"

"How did you do it?"

The praise was generous. "You even look thinner. You couldn't do that in a day."

"It took more than a day. This is Gloria's project," Miss Stein said. "It shows you what planning can do."

Gloria was far from being a model beauty, but she had certainly changed. María Luisa looked around The Club. Steve had changed too; he looked much the same, but now when he spoke, he said what he thought, not what his brother had said. Peter had changed, too, as if planning the city had touched off a live spark within him.

"What about me?" she thought. "Have I changed, too? I wonder. . . ."

CHAPTER TWENTY-SEVEN

During the next week everyone was invited to read and explain his project. It took only five minutes for the first volunteer and then everyone wanted to be next. Some of the projects might be only two paragraphs long, but everyone had something to say. About cities or club-houses, or private apartments where swimming pools replaced bathtubs and the walls were lined with fur; a chinchilla farm for Jesús in the middle of the Mission District, a wardrobe for Riko and a kitchen for Ruth.

"I done all my writing. I don' wanna do no more," Alex said.

"Maybe it's the spring. Spring fever," Peter commented.

"Could be," Miss Stein said, "but I hope you'll all spring back for just one more thing. It won't have to be long, but I'd like to ask you all to do it. Are any of you prophetic? I mean, can any of you see into the future?"

What was Miss Stein trying to say? She explained.

"All right. You'll have to close your eyes and think very

hard. I want you to see yourself five years from now. That will be your last year in high school for some of you, or perhaps some of you will be out. I want you to look in that crystal ball and describe yourself."

"Aw, Miss Stein, that's not fair."

"It's impossible!"

"How should we know?"

A series of groans followed. "You think nothing of visualizing a whole city, or a school, or tearing down half of San Francisco and building it up again. But when I ask you for something simple, what happens to you? You groan!"

The objections were hardly serious. Everyone was riding high. Everyone was feeling good, laughing and talking. Only María Luisa was baffled. The scenes that passed in front of her vision were all so conflicting that for the first time in a long time, she could not think of anything to say. Even after the others had quieted down and begun to write, she sat there biting her pencil. For a moment she closed her eyes and then decided to let the pencil write whatever came to mind.

MARíA LuisA is grownup and very beautiful, Like elena. She is dressed in the Latest Fashoin, whatever that will be, And she has MAny Freinds. I see her stepping into A white MG with a young MAN, They will be going out for the evening.

That picture faded quickly. It was too ridiculous even to dream about. She decided she must be more practical. Realistic.

I AM supposed to go back to SAN Luis, but I cANNot see myself there, Not even for a second, in the iMAginAry glAss. I cAN see MY Mother coMing here And she, MY brother and I will Live together, it would be A MiRALce, but I cAN aLMost beLeive it.

I see MYself, A Little tALLer, A Little stRAighteR. A tune sings itself in MY eArs And will Not go awAy, "I wANt to be, I wANt to be, I wANt be," it sAys over And over. But what is it I wANt to be? To go to school without cAring, to work in A Factory or A store without cAring? ~~to~~ ~~toor~~ To get MARRied And have bAbies One After another? None of that is enough For Me. Then what is? The Picture is paLe and~~f~~ then it fades,

The next day Miss Stein asked to speak with her for a few minutes after class. They sat on the stiff oak chairs of the sewing room, facing one another.

"I read your prophecy. Can't you really guess what you want to be doing?"

María Luisa looked at her shyly and said nothing.

"Why don't you say it, María Luisa?"

"That I want to write? It sounds so conceited. And foolish too. Sure, I like to make stories and poems. But I hardly passed the English course. My compositions come back with angry red corrections all over them. I think that maybe I fool myself."

"María Luisa, I've been reading your stories for several months now. I don't put red marks all over them. Writing correctly is something you can learn. Having something to say is what's important."

"What do I have to say?"

"Whatever happens to you, whatever is your experience, is what you have to say. It will be different from what anyone else has to say. There is only one María Luisa Santos. What she is or does is unique, but if you can write it, then people will understand it."

María Luisa sat perfectly still, her eyes never leaving Miss Stein's.

"Did you know there are many splendid Latin American writers, and new ones are springing up all the time in Mexico and all over South America. In some countries, like Brazil, for instance, writing poetry is a tradition. A woman from Chile, Gabriela Mistral, even won the Nobel Prize one year for her poetry."

"Why didn't I know this?" María Luisa asked.

"Next year you will find out about these writers when you study Latin American culture. Then you won't feel as alone as you feel now. You'll know that you are right in putting down what is exciting to you, like that poem you wrote about the eclipse."

"Nobody but you has ever read what I've done. Once

154

Mike found a poem and used it for a song. Nobody else, not even Peter, sees what I do."

"It's natural for writers to feel lonely. Do you feel less lonely when someone reads your work?"

María Luisa nodded. But then she couldn't go around handing her poems out.

"If you will let me, I think I could send your poems to a magazine that is interested in the work of very young writers. I can't make any promises. But I'll try to send in something. Can you bring me a few copies?"

María Luisa nodded. It was almost too exciting. She looked into her future and saw a green light saying GO and then another green light and then another, all urging her to move ahead.

Peter was waiting for her outside. "It took you long enough. What the heck were you talking about?"

She grinned.

"Come on, tell me."

"I'm starving. Why don't we get some ice cream?" she asked, deliberately changing the subject. Some things were meant to remain secret like a pearl within an oyster.

CHAPTER TWENTY-EIGHT

On a soft afternoon at the end of April, Miss Stein, in a new fern-green dress, told The Club that she had a little announcement to make. This was the last week of The Club. There was a chorus of groans and protests.

"Why? Don't you like us any more?"

"You can't leave like that, Miss Stein. You just can't."

"Change the rules. Say you gotta be here another month."

"Shut up, Stupe. You think she don't have somep'n better to do?"

"We'll work harder, Miss Stein. We won't goof off."

She smiled and asked for quiet. "I don't want to leave you. It's been great being with you and I've loved it. You *know* that. And you amaze me, you've all done so well. But I have exams to take, important exams!"

"*You* take exams?"

"Yes, I do. If I pass, it means I'll be able to go out and start a few more 'clubs' like this one in other schools where they need help. Anyway, you're all coming along so well, I'm not sure that you need me much longer. Can you remember back to that first class we had here?

"And look at you now!" Miss Stein continued. "You're a little less than perfect, I'll admit, but you're getting close. I'm proud of you all."

The news of Miss Stein's leaving hit everyone and the class became strangely silent. "How will I get along without her?" María Luisa wondered. "Everything was so awful before she came. Will it be like that after she leaves?" Looking around the table, she felt her fear reflected in more than one face.

Then someone made a feeble joke in order to break the silence. Peter began a discussion about baseball, obviously to keep the conversation going. It was a feeble effort and the discussion soon died. After class everyone hung around Miss Stein and walked with her to where her little car was parked.

"For heaven's sake," she cried, "don't look so mournful, all of you. We're all going to go on living, you know."

The next day there was still a hushed air over The Club. Three days more to go. After Miss Stein left, everyone went over to Louie's and sat around drinking Cokes while someone turned on the jukebox.

"Wow, is this bunch turned on!" Riko said. "We sit here like sack of rotten apples. You think that's what Miss Stein want from us?"

"So what do you think we should do, act like we're happy? Like we're glad she's goin' away?" Alex asked her.

"Riko didn't mean that, I think," Tassos spoke slowly but clearly now. "Of course we don't want to see Miss

Stein go, but is not good to cry like babies. She wants we should stand on our own two feet, not cry."

"I have an idea, a good idea," Gloria cried. It was still a shock to hear her speak; it was as though an overstuffed chair had begun to talk. Since her "project," however, she began to speak out more and more freely. "On the last day The Club meets, let's give a party for her."

"And give her flowers!" cried Riko.

"Hey, what about that?"

Peter and Alex, being natural leaders, somehow took over at that point. They did not need a vote; everybody knew as soon as Gloria suggested it, that a party was what they would have. In a short time there were offers of Japanese cookies, a generous spread of Mexican pastries, a special Greek cake from Tassos' mother and from Ralph the promise of a case of beer. He refused to say where he would get it, but what concerned The Club was that beer didn't seem right. He promised to bring soda.

"And flowers!" Riko cried again.

There was an argument about what kind. Everyone chipped in a bit of change and Riko promised a beautiful bouquet.

"Look!" María Luisa cried. "She's been spending all this time to teach us English. Maybe what she would like most is well, a letter from each one, something like that. We could put it all in a book."

The reaction to this was mixed. Ruth settled the argument by offering to decorate a beautiful folder to hold the letters, and Miss Stein would like to see something from *everyone*.

"Girls! Women!" Steve groaned.

"I'm sorry it's going to be over so soon," Peter said to

María Luisa as they walked up the hill past the little Mexican grocery. "But let's face it. Nothing ever stays the same. Since I am born, that is the one thing I know. So you have to take it with a kind of grace . . . is that the right word . . . because it's going to happen anyway. A farewell party makes a good finish."

"And to think that Gloria could see that first of all of us! *Dios mío*, when you think of what Miss Stein has does for all of us. . . ."

"And she will be doing it in other schools. So maybe we did help her a little, too, by being the guinea pigs."

But for all the brave words and the reassuring thoughts, the sadness remained with María Luisa. Her good friend would soon be leaving. As for The Club, it would dissolve. She wondered what really would happen to everyone now that they were left on their own. She wondered but did not mention it to Peter. There were some things he wouldn't quite understand.

CHAPTER TWENTY-NINE

One Saturday afternoon in May, Peter and María Luisa took a ride on a cable car to the park near the beach just below Ghirardelli Square. They walked along the waterfront and watched the few brave swimmers dash into the water. The Bay was dotted with sailboats and up above the gulls circled, their sharp raucous cries piercing the salt air.

It was a treat for the two of them to be out together. Peter's mother usually wanted her son to spend Saturdays with her, but today she had other things to do. So they were free.

"Do you miss The Club very much?" Peter asked María Luisa.

"Not so much when I'm with you," she said, "but there is something a little funny. I knew I would miss Miss Stein, but I didn't know I would miss the other kids so much. You know, I worry about them. Ralph dropped out and I hear Steve's in trouble. He got busted. Sometimes I wonder . . ."

"About The Club? It helped me a lot. It helped you, too, María Luisa. We could hardly talk together at first."

"I know. That Miss Stein was good for all of us. It's just that I think of my friends and what's happening to us all, and I think maybe we need something more, another kind of club."

It didn't seem to concern Peter, and María Luisa could tell there was something else on his mind, something that must be pleasant. "What is it, Peter?" she asked. He could not seem to restrain a smile.

"I have something to show you first," he said. "Want to come?"

She walked with him up the hill to the large complex of handsome shops in the old Ghirardelli chocolate factory. He led her through a plaza with a fountain and planters blooming with brilliant flowers.

"It's very nice," she said. "Is this what you want to show me?"

"Not yet," he said, and he led her to a store where Mexican products were sold. They stood in front of the window and looked at the skillful display of crafts inside, black pottery, mirrors in elaborate tin frames, handmade jewelry and woven *sarapes*. It was one of these that stopped María Luisa with surprise, because it seemed so familiar. It was a large brown serape with a pattern of brilliant moths woven in the design.

"Shall we go in?" Peter asked.

Her instinctive answer was no. "It's much too expensive and well, you go in, Peter, and I'll wait here."

"Don't be silly. They want people to come in."

She followed reluctantly but stayed very close to Peter. Fortunately there was a crowd of well-dressed people inside, and nobody asked María Luisa if they could wait on her. She edged up close to the serape and noticed the price tag.

"Peter, that's eighty dollars! Can you imagine?"

A salesman, a slender young man with a razor-thin mustache made his way over with a customer, a lady who was interested in that very serape.

"This particular pattern is an old one and a very good one. Unfortunately it's disappearing, so this is quite a find," he said. As the lady examined it, María Luisa thought the salesman was glaring at her, so she squeezed Peter's hand and they both left.

"Peter, I know why it's so familiar. It's like the old serape *Abuelita* keeps on the trunk in my room. It's old and dirty, but I think it's the very same thing!"

"Then it's valuable?"

"Maybe. I'd never give it up. I love it. I was only thinking how it's a shame nobody cares about it. The cat sleeps on it. The kids make a tent out of it when they play. Yet that Anglo lady admired it. Even I could see how beautiful it was. Was that your surprise?"

"María Luisa, how would *I* know about *your* serape? No, I just thought you would dig that store. Here, let's sit down."

They sat on a bench and Peter told her, "I'm going to be fourteen next week and my mother said I could make a party or whatever. So I said I want most of all for you to come with both of us to a Chinese restaurant. What do you say?"

Her eyes opened wide. "Wow, I would *love* it!"

But then she began to think. Would Uncle Emilio let her go? It was all right those few times when Aunt Rosa had invited Peter to stay for dinner and everybody found out he was a nice kid; even Mike liked him. But for María Luisa to really go out, even with Mrs. Jensen there? That might be a different side of the coin.

"Keep your fingers crossed," she told him, "because I have to ask my uncle."

"He'll let you go with me," Peter beamed, and his smile was so winning, María Luisa did not know how he could refuse.

CHAPTER THIRTY

One could never be sure of anything, Mara Luisa decided. She had feared what Uncle Emilio might say, but he had given his approval without hesitation, particularly when he knew Mrs. Jensen was taking them. It was Aunt Rosa who objected. "It is too serious if the mother goes, too. You are too little, too young. You are just a child, María Luisa."

In the end after a long discussion during which María Luisa came close to tears, they decided they would let her go this once. Peter was a boy they could trust. Besides, it was his birthday.

María Luisa squealed with happiness. She couldn't have stood it if they'd said no.

"I'll wear that beautiful pink dress you made me for Easter!" she promised as she hugged her aunt.

"I hope it will all turn out as well as you think," Aunt Rosa said. Her face looked clouded, and this bothered María Luisa. She wanted Aunt Rosa to approve all the way. "Oh, well, she's old-fashioned," she told herself as she tried not to think of it. It was Peter's birthday and she was going to have a good time.

Aunt Rosa was pleased nevertheless that María Luisa wanted to wear the pink dress she had made for her. María Luisa had had a difficult time convincing her aunt it must be simple, like Miss Stein's clothes, and although Aunt Rosa would have preferred more lace and ruffles, she made the dress exactly as María Luisa wanted.

On the evening of the celebration, Elena helped María Luisa dress. She insisted on giving her the slightest suspicion of makeup around the eyes and a touch of her best perfume. "You don't want to overdo it," Elena warned, a strange statement coming from her. But Elena had changed. Now she got along very well with her cousin. A new boy friend was responsible, a serious young man who expected Elena to be perfect.

Looking into the mirror, María Luisa saw a very excited girl who told herself, "Be good tonight. Keep calm. Don't act scared, Peter won't like it. Remember to say how-do-you-do to his mother. *Dios mío*, don't say *Dios mío* or any Spanish words at all. Don't speak with an accent tonight. Don't forget your table manners."

The little boys sat on her bed and watched her. *Abuelita* came in and nodded her head. "*Muy bonita!*" Was she very pretty, María Luisa wondered? Mike stopped at the door to look in and soon the whole family was crowded in the tiny bedroom to see that María Luisa was at her best.

Peter, a little stiff in his best suit, came at seven on the dot. Everyone stood around watching as María Luisa greeted him and gave him his present, a tiny package wrapped in white tissue. There was an awkward moment as they stood together, embarrassed and glowing in their best clothes. It seemed to María Luisa that they took forever, but finally they said good-bye and gratefully left the house.

CHAPTER THIRTY-ONE

"How nice you look! You are all dressed up."

"You too."

"I wish I had my jeans on. But my mother insisted on these. So here I am."

"It looks nice," María Luisa said to make him feel better, although she would have felt more comfortable in her skirt and he seemed more natural in jeans. Where was his mother, she wondered.

"If you don't mind, my mother is not quite ready. We can walk over to the apartment and by that time she should be all dressed."

It was the first time María Luisa had been in the Jensen apartment. It was in fact the first time she had been in a home that was not that of Chicanos. The Jensen apartment was not far away, but it looked over a different section of the city and that somehow made a great deal of difference.

"It's a lovely home, Peter. Like a picture in a magazine," she whispered, impressed by the thick blue rug on the floor, the light wooden furniture, and the circle of eight delicate blue plates placed on the white wall. She found herself fascinated by them.

"They are from Denmark," Peter explained, "and all the Danes are proud of them. Each year my mother gets a new one. It's a kind of family treasure."

Then Peter showed her the small model of the wooden ship that his father had once made; it was the ship on which his father was an officer. He explained modestly that the brightly woven pillows had been made by his grandmother and the pewter candlesticks had come from Denmark.

"You must be proud to have so many fine things," she said. She had not noticed that Peter's mother had come in and had been watching her. Now she came over to her.

"So you must be María Luisa, Peter's little friend! He's told me how much you have helped him with his English. I'm afraid he speaks better than I do."

María Luisa, confused, could not quite agree or disagree without hurting someone, so she smiled and whispered a barely audible "how-do-you-do." Peter's mother was charming, absolutely charming, like no mother María Luisa had ever seen. She was blond and slender and seemed more like Peter's older sister than his mother. It was not until later on that evening that María Luisa noticed the small wrinkles around her eyes and a tightness in her throat that betrayed her age. Yet, even as she rushed up to María Luisa and took her hand, her first impression was one of coldness, as though a cool breeze had come in.

"It's Peter's choice tonight because it's his birthday. I hope you like Chinatown," Mrs. Jensen chattered in a polite way to cover up the gap in the conversation, for both Peter and María Luisa seemed to have been struck dumb. "Maybe we'd better start," she said.

"Hold on a minute, Mother," Peter said. "María Luisa's given me a present and I'll die of curiosity if I don't open it. May I ?" he asked María Luisa, who blushed. After the elegant things in the Jensen apartment, she was ashamed of her simple gift, a small peace sign on a chain; it had seemed good-looking in the store and she had had to borrow two dollars from Mike to pay for it. Now in Peter's hand it looked so tiny, she wanted to cry.

"It's great, exactly what I wanted!" Peter said as he put it around his neck.

"Yes, it's lovely, dear, but really we should go," said his mother. "It's getting late."

They rode to Chinatown in a Volkswagen, Peter sitting with his mother in front while María Luisa bounced around in back. The hills terrified her. Aside from Miss Summer's old Chevy which had often bounced María Luisa along the Arizona back roads, María Luisa had been in very few cars. If the San Francisco hills were frightening, they were nothing compared to the five-story parking lot that Mrs. Jensen entered so confidently, driving expertly up the curving ramp that led to the top story where she parked the car. "She is so capable, I shouldn't be afraid," María Luisa said to herself. It was not Mrs. Jensen's driving, however, but something else that warned her to be careful.

Grant Avenue, the main street of Chinatown, was a great jam of people, shops, and enormous cars blowing their horns impatiently in the crowded streets. Peter clutched her hand tightly as it would be easy to get separated. Thousands of tourists seemed to amble along and almost as many Chinese were weaving their way in and out of the crowds. Cars could not pass, yet a truck blaring out Chinese songs and speeches managed to speed through. Lights, lanterns, waving banners, and fragments of conversation in Chinese and English made it a confusion of noise and color. It was almost like being in a foreign country.

"Do you like it?" Peter asked.

She grinned and nodded, loving its excitement, but she could say nothing because Mrs. Jensen was quickly leading them through the crowds, down a side street and up a flight of stairs to a restaurant. It was an old restaurant with dark varnished tables and quiet orange lights. Mrs. Jensen followed a waiter to a table, indicated a chair for María Luisa, and then sat with Peter opposite her. "That's so we can both look at that cute little friend of yours," she explained although she seemed to be speaking to Peter. Her smile was chilly.

A waiter brought tea and menus, but one sight of the menu left María Luisa more confused than ever at the

Chinese characters. Even the English menu at the bottom did not help. She couldn't tell what any of the dishes might be.

"Shall we order for you, dear?" Mrs. Jensen's voice made her feel like a very stupid little child, but she had no choice but to say, "If you don't mind." Then Mrs. Jensen and Peter discussed the menu, argued over the best combination of foods. María Luisa did not know what they said, but she knew that they understood each other perfectly, and she felt more than ever like a stranger. After the waiter took their order, Mrs. Jensen looked at María Luisa.

"Peter told me your mother is ill. I'm sorry."

"Yes, but she's getting better. She's nearly well."

"I suppose you'll be going back to New Mexico then."

"Not New Mexico. Arizona. Only I think perhaps my mother might come here because her family is here."

"Oh, I see," she said with a finality that ended the conversation. What does she see? María Luisa thought, puzzled by Peter's mother. Then Peter changed the subject. "Want to see something great? Watch that family over there."

Several tables had been put together and a large family with many children were sitting around, chattering in Chinese and pecking expertly with chopsticks at what seemed to be hundreds of different serving dishes. What a good time they were having, all of them, the children, the grown-ups and even the old grandparents who sat with them! All that joking and laughing and chattering and a moment of sympathy while a tiny child reached for a shrimp that was far away and brought it to his plate triumphantly at the end of his chopsticks . . . it was all in

Chinese, yet it reminded María Luisa of some of the parties at Aunt Rosa's.

"Perhaps it's a birthday party," she said and was immediately sorry. They were having such fun and Peter's birthday celebration was so strained. Poor Peter!

The dinner was disastrous. It wasn't that the steaming colorful dishes that the waiter brought were not fascinating, but there was no silverware, only chopsticks. She watched Peter and his mother as they piled their plates and handled their long polished sticks perfectly. Then Peter realized what was wrong.

"You've never used these? I'm sorry, I should have told you. Hold them like this, between your fingers. You'll catch on," he said. As he helped her hold the chopsticks, he squeezed her hand as if to say "have courage." If only the two of them were there together, it would have been so much fun, María Luisa thought. As it was, María Luisa was so afraid of dropping a bit of meat or a luscious pink shrimp on the table, that she ate very little.

Mrs. Jensen talked constantly because Peter and María Luisa seemed to have lost their voices. Mrs. Jensen talked about the year she and Peter lived in Paris, that odd Christmas they had spent in Spain another time, and some of the places they hoped to go to soon. The phrase "Peter and I—," "Peter and I—" seemed to repeat itself over and over until María Luisa did not hear the stories, only the insistent "Peter and I—."

At last the meal was over and Mrs. Jensen chatted in a false cheery voice all the way home. When the car pulled up in front of the Nuñez house, Peter told his mother he would see María Luisa to the door and then walk home by himself. She began to object, but something stern in Peter's voice surprised her, so she said, "Well, all right, darling!" and drove off.

"María Luisa, I'm sorry. I had no idea it would be so dreadful for you. You looked so tiny sitting there. Well, I apologize for my mother."

"Don't, Peter. I think I understand. She loves you and wanted to be alone with you on your birday. You should never say bad things about your mother."

At the same time she was thinking that although her mother was not the fine-looking lady Mrs. Jensen was, she would never have behaved so unkindly. It made María Luisa feel only a little better to know this. She had expected a birthday party, not a contest between Peter's mother and her. And there was Peter looking disconsolate.

"Don't look so unhappy, Peter. It's your birthday. I wish now I had made a birthday cake for you with lots of candles."

He put his arms around her and kissed her.

"María Luisa, you're the nicest girl I have ever known anywhere. I was very lonely until I met you."

"Me too."

They stood there holding hands until Aunt Rosa's voice floated down from above. This time it was very quiet, almost a whisper.

"Time to come in now, María Luisa. Happy birthday, Peter."

"Thanks," he called up to Aunt Rosa, pleased that she liked him so directly and easily.

"Good night, Peter."

171

"Good night, María Luisa!"

He walked away looking very tall, very young, and very much alone.

CHAPTER THIRTY-TWO

The next two weeks Peter was the Peter María Luisa knew so well, a Peter who was full of smiles and jokes, who argued about politics furiously, a Peter who sang as they walked home from school. Then one day he said almost nothing and for the next few days remained quiet.

"What's the matter, Peter? You might as well tell me. I know something is wrong."

"I don't want to tell you now."

"Tell me what? It's not like you to be like this."

He stopped right there on the sidewalk. "All right, I'll tell you. As soon as school is over, we're moving down to L.A."

"You're moving away?" Her lips moved and she could think of nothing more to say.

"You met my mother, so now you should know that when she makes up her mind to move, we move. Do you know how many places I have lived in, how many different schools I have gone to? It's always the same excuse. We'll see my father more. She'll get a better job. I'll go to a better school."

"I thought you were happy here. You have that beautiful apartment."

"We were, as happy as we ever get."

"You don't want to go, do you?"

He shook his head. "Of course not. My mother wants to give the idea that we are Beautiful People or something, always moving around; it sounds so good when you say it. I tell you, it's terrible. I make a friend, and that's when we have to leave. I don't belong anywhere."

"So she wants you to move this time because of me. Is that right?"

Peter's face grew red and he did not answer. So María Luisa knew it was true. For a moment she remembered Carol Kraus and the shock of finding out that Carol hated her without even knowing her. Peter's mother was the same way. She was beginning to understand now and was no longer surprised, only saddened.

"I know about these things, Peter. Your mother doesn't want you to go with a Chicano."

"Well, that's my mother's problem, not mine. I'll go with anyone I like," he cried angrily. His voice became calmer as he continued. "I think about it and think about it all the time. There's not so much I can do now. Someday, when I'm old enough, I'll leave my mother, and I would leave her, too, for something like this. But it's not time yet."

They walked together slowly. Too realistic to say "We'll meet again," or "I'll come back," or "I'll always wait for you," which is what they say in movies, they knew they would be separated soon and that would probably be the end.

"We have one month together, almost thirty days, and then we leave," he said.

"I thought it was the end of the world when Miss Stein left. This is even worse."

"We don't have much choice, do we?"

"No. We're not little children and we're not grown-up either. Still, think if we hadn't met! There'd be a great big hole in my life. So I'm grateful."

They were standing at the stairs that led to the Nuñez house. Children played in the street, and from above came the sounds of Mike's guitar. He was playing one of his own compositions, a slow sad song; from time to time he stopped to correct a chord or sing along with his guitar. The sounds filled the air.

"That music says things I could never put in words," María Luisa said.

"You don't need words. I can see in your eyes what you feel, what you want to say."

They held hands. Below them stretched the city, its white houses strung out in lines over the hills. Everything was stained orange in the glow of the setting sun and before their eyes, the color deepened and changed to violet. They did not know how long they had been standing there, only that each moment had become precious.

"I'll see you tomorrow," he said as Aunt Rosa's voice calling Juan, José, and María Lueeeeees-sa spilled into the twilight. Peter kissed her quickly and disappeared down the street.

CHAPTER THIRTY-THREE

Thirty days! Exciting days! María Luisa never knew it was possible to be happy and sad all at once.

The good news was that her mother was well and would be coming to San Francisco! Letters flew back and forth between San Luis and San Francisco as plans took shape. Miss Summer had agreed it would be better for Mrs. Santos to live in San Francisco as the children were going to school there and besides Mrs. Santos's family lived there. Miss Summer had written a letter to Aunt Rosa and María Luisa warning them that Mrs. Santos was not as strong as she might be and they should look after her and see that she had plenty of rest.

"Then we must have our own place, Aunt Rosa. We have already crowded you too much."

"Don't say such a thing! You and Juan and your mother are always welcome to make a home with us. It is our pleasure. Only I think your mother will need to rest and with so many people coming and going, the noisy little boys, and Rosita, perhaps we'd better find a place for you after all."

175

With all the houses in San Francisco, María Luisa thought it would be easy to find a place to live, a place that was nice, clean, and cheap. *Caray!* She had a lot to learn. Aunt Rosa looked around for apartments during the day while her niece was at school and told her about them each night.

"You like this place, María Luisa?" she would ask in a doubtful tone of voice. María Luisa knew immediately that the dark windowless apartment would never do for an invalid coming from such a sunny place as San Luis, and Aunt Rosa would agree they must look further for a place that would be light and airy.

"It's not easy," Aunt Rosa cried.

But she found such a place. A perfect place. Aunt Rosa and María Luisa planned how they would put a bed here and a table there and then they asked the rent. Incredible! Did they really mean it? How could anyone ask for so much money?

"Never mind," Aunt Rosa said. "You have a little more school so think of your schoolwork, and I know you want to be with Peter. We'll find something. I'll look every day."

The joy in Aunt Rosa's eyes as she talked about her sister was nothing compared to the joy and relief María Luisa felt. Her mother was well and coming to be with them! Juan was more excited than anyone. With each letter from San Luis, he literally jumped up and down with joy or rolled on the floor laughing.

"You're a silly little puppy dog, that's what you are!" María Luisa would cry as she hugged him.

Every day he asked, when is she coming, how many

days now, will we meet her at the bus? But nobody could become angry with him. They were all too happy.

Never had thirty days been so sad either. Peter and María Luisa saw each other every chance they had. They met in the halls briefly between classes. They ate lunch in the schoolroom together or sometimes with Riko and Ruth. They took long walks after school.

One afternoon Peter was waiting for her outside the school, a blond boy in a blue sweater, a boy with blue eyes staring into a blue sky.

"What's been keeping you, María Luisa?"

"I met Alex in the hall. I hadn't seen him for some time. We talked a little. That's all."

Peter nodded his head and talked of other things. But María Luisa did not tell him what she and Alex had talked about. They had talked in Spanish.

"Hi, María Luisa, it's been a long time. How are you?"

"Great. And you?"

"So-so. Spending all your time with Peter? I hear he's going away."

"Soon," she didn't want to talk about Peter. It hurt too much. "Do you miss The Club, Alex?"

"Who, me? Not very much. That Miss Stein was pretty nice; she did what she could. I'm in another club now. A Chicano club."

"A Chicano club? What's that?" she asked, interested.

"It's a sort of teen club—nothing to do with school. Just a place. You know that store on Mission with the orange curtains? That's it."

"I think I saw the place. What do you do there?"

"Talk. Think. Dance. Play music. You keep in touch. Look, wanna come down sometime?"

"Yes, I really would. I can't for a while, but later on I think I'd like to see what it's like," she said. There had been no need to mention that she would not go while Peter was still around, but Alex understood.

"I'll see you around," he said and then she hurried to meet Peter.

They walked with a silence between them. They climbed a hill past a green park where little children played in a sandpit while their mothers sat on benches and talked together. A man selling Good Humor bars came by with his little wagon and Peter bought some. It was a day like any other day, but it had a number on it, a number that would mean one day less than thirty.

"There's not much time left. . . ."

"Peter, let's not spoil it by thinking of it so much. If we talk about separating all the time, then it won't seem as though we were together at all."

"Right!" At that moment they were passing a record store and there was a record Peter wanted to hear, a disc by one of his favorite folksingers. They went in, Peter asked for the record, and the two sat together in a little glass booth and held hands as they listened.

The singer's voice was quiet and mellow; the guitar accompanying him was haunting in its harmonies. But all the songs, every last one, was about love and sorrow and the sadness of parting!

Peter and María Luisa looked at each other and finally laughed. For all their good intentions, there was no escaping the subject.

"It's fate!" they cried at the same time, but Peter

bought the record anyway. "It will always make me think of you," he said.

They spent every day together and Saturday and Sunday afternoons. They walked through the Park, along the beach or through the city as they had done so many times before.

Then there came a day when they took off their shoes and walked in the sand beside the ocean. They said little. They stopped to watch the sandpipers run along the beach in front of the waves and they admired some dogs that ran along the beach with their masters. Peter found a perfect shell and gave it to María Luisa; she found three sand dollars and gave them to him. Eventually they put on their shoes and walked home, earlier than usual. Peter and his mother had been invited out to dinner on their last night in San Francisco.

They stood in front of the house for the last time. They cried a little. It was really good-bye and there was nothing they could do about it. They embraced; they kissed; and then Peter walked away.

CHAPTER THIRTY-FOUR

Late in June, Mike, Juan, and María Luisa went to the bus station to wait for Mrs. Santos. They smiled at each other and nobody said anything but each remembered the time they had last been at the station when they had gone to look for Juan. María Luisa thought too about her own arrival in San Francisco. She had been so frightened and the station had seemed so enormous. Now it did not seem so large at all.

At last the bus came in, an hour late, and the three of them waited tensely until Mrs. Santos appeared, the last passenger to get off. "It's like her to let everyone else go first," María Luisa said. How tiny her mother seemed as she hesitated on the step! María Luisa had always thought of her as being big, an adult. Now she seemed small and delicate, the large eyes darker than ever and the black hair pulled back neatly.

They made their way to her as fast as they could through the crowd and embraced her. Juan would not stop kissing her. How wonderful to be together again! Tears of happiness spilled over. María Luisa's fingers felt how thin her mother was as she embraced her, and with this came the realization that from now on she would have to take care of her.

"Let me look at you! My, how you have grown! María Luisa, you're a young lady now. And Juan, what a big boy! Let's see, this is Miguel?"

"Yes, I'm Miguel," he said as he kissed her on the cheek.

"Is this your suitcase?" he asked, as he was about to carry it for her.

"Yes. It's brand-new. Miss Summer and Sister Celeste gave it to me. They send their love."

Mike said he was going to get a taxi.

"It's too expensive," María Luisa whispered.

"That's what money is for, occasions like this. Anyway, your mother looks a little tired," he said.

The homecoming was a funny thing. Everyone laughed and cried and hugged one another, all at once. There was so much to say that everyone spoke at once. Memories sprang up; questions about the future and thoughts saved up for years came rushing out.

On that first night there was a simple family dinner, for María Luisa's mother was tired from the trip and needed to rest.

On Saturday night there was a big party. Mrs. Santos

sat there pale and happy, like a little queen, while people kept coming to see her and welcome her. Mike's combo was there playing in her honor; every once in a while someone had to shout, "Softer, Mike, for the love of God, softer!" Kids ran in and out dressed in their best clothes, the little boys with sparkling white shirts and the little girls in frothy pink dresses. Juan and José with as much self-consciousness as pride, performed a little ritual they had learned in school from their beautiful new teacher. Standing side by side, a wide grin displaying the open space in José's mouth where he had lost his front teeth, they lifted their arms and said:

"I am big. I am handsome. I am proud to be a Chicano."

Everyone applauded. Mrs. Santos had never heard of children doing such things in school but it must be good, for the boys were growing straight and tall.

While the party went on, María Luisa saw her mother in a way she had never seen her before. In the past her mother was someone who was there to take care of her. Now María Luisa saw her as a person in her own right, a remarkable woman. She had had a childhood of unbelievable poverty, ten people living in two miserable rooms and a father who could not find work. She married young, and her husband took her away from her family. He could be kind, but he beat her when he was drunk. She had lost three babies. Then she lost her husband in a terrible truck accident. As if that weren't enough trouble, she had become gravely ill and had to be separated from her children.

Yet here she was, ready to start a new life in a new place, and her eyes were filled with hope. María Luisa was proud of her and proud to be her daughter.

For all that María Luisa was grateful that her mother had come to live with her and Juan, she felt oddly lost. When Peter left, it was as though part of her own life had been torn away and no amount of sensible thinking seemed to help. She decided it was better to have known him even though it meant suffering later than never to have met him. Still, an agonizing restlessness plagued her. Finding it too trying to stay at home with her mother and Aunt Rosa every evening and pretend everything was all right, she began to take long walks so that she would come home exhausted and fall asleep immediately and not have to think of how she missed Peter.

One sultry evening in early July as she came up Mission Street after one of her long walks, she passed a small storefront with orange cheesecloth curtains. She thought she heard the faint sounds of a guitar and she knew she heard many voices. When she was half a block past it, she realized this was the club or meeting place that Alex had told her about. She retraced her steps and opened the door cautiously.

"Come in, come in," a young man called out. "Find a seat anywhere. We're just rapping."

The room was filled with young people sitting on the sofas or the floor. As she paused looking for a place where she could sit, someone called out, "Hey, it's María Luisa! Hi!" Ralph! She found herself smiling, grateful to find a familiar face. A girl with a wide soft face, a girl María Luisa had liked immediately, moved to make room, and María Luisa sat on the floor between her and an intense young man who might have been eighteen.

The young man, Carlos, was talking about the job situation and he seemed to know what jobs were available and where they could be found, although at best it was a discouraging situation. María Luisa liked the way he talked and she liked the way he listened whenever anyone else had something to say. She looked around the room at the young people sitting there; they were all ages, from twelve to twenty, maybe older, but age did not seem to make much difference. Studying their faces, the earnest ones, the subdued ones, the faces that revealed the dreamers and those with deep troubles, she began to feel the restlessness subside and a new warmth take its place.

During a short break she talked with the girl with the wide face. She told María Luisa in Spanish that she had just come from Texas and would begin school in the fall. María Luisa could feel in her an eagerness and a fear and she understood it well. "I was like that, too," she thought. Then she wondered if she and this girl, Anna, would be friends. Maybe she would be able to help her.

As she walked home later, words formed themselves in her mind and made everything clear. "These are my people and I'm at home when I am with them," they said. Then she sighed; it had taken her long enough to find out, but now she knew this was so.

One day toward the end of July, Elena handed a thick envelope to María Luisa. It had just come in the mail.

"It's from your Miss Stein," Elena said.

With trembling fingers María Luisa opened the envelope and pulled out a note in Miss Stein's even writing:

Dear María Luisa:

Congratulations! You'll find one of your poems printed in the copy of Journal for young writers. I hope you will send more of your poems and stories to the Journal.

Do you ever see members of the Club? It was a fine group. I enjoyed knowing you all and I hope it was worthwhile.

Keep on writing, María Luisa. I think you have something to say. Good luck to you and much love,

Judith Stein

Her heart raced as she read the note over and over. What a friend she had been, what a very good friend! Then she looked through the *Journal*, and sure enough, there was her poem and her name in print.

María Luisa's mother was more than proud and Aunt Rosa said she always expected great things from María Luisa. But it was Uncle Emilio who amazed her. He was proudest of all, and his praise was so lavish that María Luisa turned red with embarrassment. He even wanted to take the *Journal* to work with him so that he could show off his niece in front of his friends.

María Luisa confessed to her mother, "For someone who thinks girls should think only of being wives and mothers, Uncle Emilio is acting strange. I wonder if I'll ever understand adults."

In August, thanks to Aunt Rosa and a bit of good luck, the Santoses moved into their own apartment. It was very small, but then there were only three in the family. To begin with it was very dark and although the landlord refused to paint it, Aunt Rosa bothered him until he bought the paint; then Mike, Elena, and María Luisa painted the walls a fresh clean white. Mrs. Santos, whose embroidery and needlework were as fine as her sister's, was going to be able to do some work at home, and was glad for the little sunlight that came through the living-room window.

"It's beautiful," María Luisa said to herself over and over. The few pieces of furniture they needed came from the Goodwill store, and she had painted them a clear pale blue. Three Mexican plates decorated with birds and flowers hung proudly on one wall. On another was the serape which *Abuelita* insisted on giving to María Luisa. Mrs.

Santos had begun to grow plants and herbs in pots on the kitchen windowsill and María Luisa knew that as soon as she could, she would buy her mother a canary in a cage.

And at last, María Luisa had a room of her own. It was a very tiny room with a single window, very tall and narrow.

Late one Saturday night in August, María Luisa sat at the wooden table that served as her desk. She had just come back from a birthday party at the Chicano center, but she wasn't sleepy, not yet. As she looked out at the dazzling city that seemed to lay at her feet, it occurred to her that although the next building blocked some of the view, still the view was wider than before.

"*Caray,*" she said, "I think I begin to understand."

ABOUT THE AUTHOR

Winifred Madison was born in Rhode Island but was raised in Hartford, Connecticut, which she considers her home. She attended Mt. Holyoke, and continued her studies at the University of California, graduating Phi Beta Kappa in 1964. She is married to a professor of botany and they have four children. Mrs. Madison is especially interested in art, particularly batik wall hangings, and the social problems that confront children of ethnic backgrounds. This is Mrs. Madison's first book.